I0626174

Dadtime Stories
Douglas Schwartz

v1.0

ISBN—978-0-9860554-6-1

www.checkeredscissors.com

Published in 2025 by Douglas Schwartz

Copyright © 2025 by Douglas Schwartz

Stories by Douglas Schwartz
Cover art by Douglas Schwartz

TABLE OF CONTENTS

Prologue

Mom heads out of town for training for her new job.

Dad is a single parent for the first time over four days.

This is the story of their kids, Danny and Liz...

...and of their first encounter with...

Dadtime Stories.

Eight year old Danny Montgomery sat at the kitchen table eating dry cereal from a plastic bowl decorated with a cartoon cow. Still half asleep, he groggily watched his mom, Ellie, frantically flit around the house, grabbing her daily vitamins from the pantry, her earphones from the coffee table, her half-read mystery novel from the end table, and anything else she might need for her business trip.

Ellie had recently started a new job, which meant the company needed her to complete a few days of training at the company's headquarters. If the training was in town, Ellie would not be leaving the kids alone with Dad for four days, but the head office was not even in the same state.

The more things Ellie forgot to pack, like granola bars for both flights or the spare floss from the half-bathroom, the more she crammed into her already overstuffed suitcase and carry-on bag. Danny hoped Mom still had room to bring something back for him and his younger sister, Liz.

At age five, Liz wanted to get as much attention from Mom before she left. Liz picked an inopportune time to show Mom her latest crayon artwork.

Danny wanted more Momtime, too, but remained at the table munching on his chocolatey puffed cereal in a sleepy haze. He knew Mom was going away for a while, but the thought of her being away had not sunk in this early in the morning. As much as he would miss Mom, Danny knew it was best to keep out of her way. He stayed at the kitchen table until he knew when it was safe to approach her.

His dad, Ben, also knew to stay out of Ellie's way, and deflected Liz from Mom as much as possible until Ellie was ready to go. He tried to keep Liz on track to get ready for school by reminding her to brush her teeth and pack her school bag. Ellie usually was frantic moments before leaving on family

3

vacations, and this was no exception. Ben also kept Ellie focused while absorbing all the last minute details flowing from his wife.

"Remember to check their bags for homework and notices from the school," Ellie told Ben.

"Got it."

"And Ben, remember they each get one vitamin in the mornings only. Just because they look like gummy bears, don't let them talk you into more at dinnertime."

"Yes, I know."

"And, make sure you check the mail. I'm expecting that check from the insurance company."

"Ellie, I've got this. I'm good," he reassured her.

Ellie stopped, held his cheek with her free hand, looked Ben in the eyes, and smiled. She said, "I know you do," but concern still shadowed her smile.

Danny could sense Mom's nervousness. He wasn't sure if she worried about traveling, her training, or about leaving Dad on his own to handle he and Liz for four days. Liz definitely looked concerned about Mom leaving. It had always been both Mom and Dad. Two parents for two kids. Over the next few days, it would be only Dad taking care of both kids. Could Dad handle both on his own? What if Mom forgot to tell Dad something important and he could not reach her because she was hundreds of miles away? What if he or Liz broke Dad while Mom was away? The reality of the situation finally sunk in. Danny squirmed in his chair.

Ben took Ellie's suitcase and carry-on into the garage to load them into the Honda Civic. Mom normally drove her Mini Cooper, but she preferred not to leave it at the airport. Dad rarely drove Mom's car. Danny wasn't sure if Dad knew how to drive Mom's car, or if Mom would even allow Dad to drive her car.

Danny watched Mom walk the house from the kitchen to the bedroom and back again. She pointed to table surfaces and mumbled about where she packed each last minute item, and whether they were in the suitcase or the carry-on.

"When is your return flight?" Ben asked, coming in from the garage.

"Late Thursday. The kids will be in bed by the time I return," she said, "Or, should be."

"Remind me, again…Whose kids are these? And what are their names?" Ben said with a grin. Ellie smirked at Ben and shook her head. Both kids protested.

"Behave for Daddy," Mom said as she hugged each of the kids.

"We will," Danny and Liz said in unison.

"And, make sure Daddy behaves, too," she said, and winked at Ben.

"He will", they said, grinning and giggling.

Ben pretended to look mischievous, and winked at Ellie.

One more quick round of hugs and kisses later, Ellie was out the door and into the car. She pulled out of the driveway and disappeared down the street with the remaining three Montgomerys waving goodbye from the driveway. With Mom gone, it was time to continue the daily routine of preparing themselves for school or work. Danny trudged upstairs to brush his teeth. He doubted their daily routine would still flow just as smoothly with only one parent.

Counting Cattle

A story about taking the time

to check for mistakes.

In the afternoon, Danny and Liz waited longer than usual to be picked up from school. They weren't the last ones to be picked up, but the number of other kids waiting to be picked up dwindled.

"Do you think Daddy got lost?" Liz wondered aloud.

"No. He knows how to find the school. He dropped us off this morning. Remember?" Danny said.

"Oh, yeah," she said, and continued looking up and down the street.

"But, maybe he forgot he needs to pick us up," Danny said.

Liz frowned and elbowed her brother in the ribs.

Liz pointed and gasped, "It's Mommy!"

The Mini Cooper pulled into the drop-off circle, surprising Danny. He thought Mom really had come back to pick them up from school. Then, he saw Dad sitting behind the wheel.

Danny opened the door and climbed into the back seat after his sister.

"Sorry, I'm late," Dad said, "There was an accident."

Danny asked, "Not Mom's car?"

"Oh, no. Not Mom's car. Another car. Lots of traffic, but, here I am," Dad said, smiling.

On the way home, Danny said, "Liz thought you got lost."

"I know how to find the school," Dad assured her.

"Told you," Danny teased.

Unable to elbow him, Liz slapped Danny's arm with the back of her hand.

They passed the scene of the accident where traffic merged to one lane, while the two banged up cars blocked the other lane. A police officer talked with both drivers near the curb.

After arriving home, Danny and Liz pulled their homework from their school bags. Dad stepped out to collect the mail from the box down the street. Before Dad got back from the mailbox, *recycled the junk mail, kicked off his shoes, and used the restroom, Danny had finished his homework. "Can I watch TV until dinner time?" Danny asked.*

Skeptical, Dad asked, "You're already finished with your homework?"

"Yep. All done. Can I watch TV?"

"That was fast. What homework did you have today?"

"Word problems. Multiplication and division. Can I watch TV?" Danny asked again, reaching for the remote.

"May I see your homework?"

Danny groaned and fetched his homework. He stomped back to Dad, flipped the piece of paper at him, and said, "Here."

Dad looked over Danny's answers and marked several of the problems with little stars.

"I think you should slow down and check your work," Dad told Danny, handing back the worksheet.

Danny groaned again and stomped back to the kitchen table where they did their homework. In the time it took Dad to empty his pocket of his wallet and some crumpled receipts, then hang up both Mom's car key and the mailbox key on the rack in the utility room, Danny came stomping back. The poorly erased smudges were evidence he had attempted to fix only two of the seven starred problems. Dad pointed out that one of the two corrections was still wrong, and he hadn't corrected the others.

"I still see some mistakes," Dad said, handing the homework back to Danny.

"Which ones?" he whined.

"I starred the ones you should look at," Dad said, indicating his marks.

Danny groaned louder and stormed back to the table. He slumped into his chair and crossed his arms. He didn't think it was fair. He did his homework. He answered all the problems.

Why couldn't he watch TV?

Dad crossed the room and sat down next to Danny at the kitchen table. Danny picked up his pencil and furiously started erasing all his answers to start all over. Dad calmly slid the homework away from him and took the pencil from Danny's hand. Dad flipped the homework face down and gently laid the pencil on top.

Danny thought this was so unfair. First, Dad wanted him to do his homework. Then, he wanted him to redo his homework. Now, he didn't want him to do it? So unfair. He wished Dad would have gone on the trip instead of Mom.

"Danny," Dad said, "I know you would rather watch cartoons than do homework, but your homework is important. And, it's important you take the time do it the right way. Okay?"

"I guess," Danny said, and reached for his homework.

Dad slid Danny's homework a little further away.

Danny raised his voice at Dad and said, "I thought you wanted me to do my homework!"

"I do, but I can tell you are upset. Take a couple of deep breaths and relax first."

Instead of taking smooth, meditative breaths, Danny breathed deep, huffing and puffing like the big, bad wolf. He asked, "May I have my homework?"

"Yes, you may," Dad said, and handed him the worksheet and pencil. "I want you to take your time and check your work. Otherwise, you will end up like Greg and his cows."

Danny picked up the pencil, looked at Dad, and asked, "Who is Greg? What does my homework have to do with cows?"

Dad said, "Let me tell you the story of Greg. He learned the hard way if he didn't take the time to do things right the first time, he could find himself in more trouble later."

COUNTING CATTLE

Once upon a time, there was a young man named Greg who moved to the country to start a ranch. He went to the market where people could buy different farm and ranch animals. There were sheep, chickens, horses, hogs, and cattle.

Most people avoided one particular rancher with a pen full of cattle much larger than the other available breeds. These particular cattle were even cheaper than the others. Greg couldn't figure out why everyone avoided the man and his spectacular herd. He overheard many people saying the breed was too much trouble to take care of. But, cows were cows. How could raising one breed be much different from raising any of the others?

Greg approached the rancher and proudly said, "I'm starting a ranch. I'd like to buy some of your cattle,"

"A fine choice, young man. How many would you like?" the rancher asked.

Greg decided to buy an even fifty, and the seller quoted him a generous price.

"You are selling some impressive cattle. I feel like I'm robbing you at that price," Greg said.

"When you see how difficult it can be to deal with this lot, you'll appreciate my bargain price and may think *I* overcharged *you*," the rancher said.

"Why are they difficult? Do they eat too much?"

"Nope. It's because of their personality. This breed of cattle tends to get into mischief."

Greg looked at the cattle in the pen. The cows just stood there chewing their cud and looking bored. What kind of trouble could a herd of cattle get into? "You're pulling my leg."

"No, sir, I am not. Are you sure you want so many? You'll need to make sure you count each and every one each and every day. Be sure to lock all of them in the barn at night, otherwise…," the old rancher trailed off and shook his head, and then added, "Just make sure you count them all, that's all I'm saying."

Greg still thought the old rancher was playing a joke on him. After he paid for the fifty cows, the old rancher counted and recounted the ones that he sold and the ones he had remaining. The old rancher wished Greg good luck after he loaded the cows into the truck to be taken to his new ranch.

The cows adjusted well to Greg's new ranch, and he soon settled into his routine. In the morning, he opened the barn to let the cows into the field. He kept them well fed and watered. Both Greg and the cows adjusted to a milking schedule. In the evening, he herded the cows back into the barn.

One night, as Greg herded the cows from the field and into the barn, he only counted forty-nine. He looked out over the field in the dim evening light and did not see any more. He tried counting the cows while they were in the barn, but they ambled around too much making it difficult to count. Instead of taking his time to count the cows again, he assumed he must have miscounted the first time and figured he must still have all fifty. Greg did not see one, sneaky cow pretending to be a boulder among a pile of rocks in the field.

In the morning, as Greg opened the barn to let his cattle into the field for the day, a white van with a red flashing light pulled onto the dirt road leading to his ranch. Sheriff Dunbar stepped out of the van and asked, "Are you missing any cattle?"

Greg looked to the line of cows coming out of the barn and meandering to the field. He thought about how he may have miscounted one cow the night before.

"I'm not sure," he said. "Maybe."

The sheriff opened the back of the van and extended a ramp. One cow hiccuped as it trotted down the ramp and joined the other cattle in the field.

"I received a call on this one. Apparently, she broke into George

Smucker's shed and drank a whole barrel of his homemade root beer. You're new in town, so I'll let this pass with a warning. I strongly suggest you keep a better eye on your cattle."

Sheriff Dunbar tipped his hat and drove away.

Greg drove out to George Smucker's place and paid him for the barrel of root beer and to replace the shed's lock and door which were both badly damaged when the cow broke in.

That evening, as Greg loaded the cows back into the barn, he only counted forty-seven cows. Knowing he did not count three cows concerned him, but his thoughts were preoccupied with how the one cow had caused such mischief. How did she get all the way out to the Smucker farm? How did she break into George's shed? And, how could she have drank an entire barrel of root beer? His thoughts were too muddled. Again, he looked out at the field in the dim evening light. He saw hay stacks, the watering trough, and a few shade trees. No cattle. Surely all his cows were in the barn.

Greg did not see two cows covered in grass pretending to be haystacks and one other cow crouched behind the watering trough.

In the morning, as the young rancher opened the barn to let his cattle into the field for the day, Sheriff Dunbar returned in his patrol car, followed by a flatbed truck hauling three of his cows.

"Oh no," Greg said. As the sheriff got out of his car, Greg asked, "Now what?"

"Well, first your cows took John Hansen's tractor for a joyride through town. They ended up at the ice cream social where they went around tipping over members of the church. I'm fining you $300, mostly to cover the dry cleaning bills. If I have to come out here one more time for your cattle, I'm hauling you in for criminal mischief."

Greg apologized for the trouble. He accepted the return of his cows, the fine, and the sheriff's second warning.

* * *

That evening, at an earlier time when there was still plenty of day light, Greg was determined to get a correct count. He counted the cows as they entered the barn. Once again, he counted a number less than fifty. He counted again, even with the difficulty of the cows ambling around the barn and resulted in the same number. He walked through the field checking every corner and found four stray cows hiding up in the trees. After ushering the cows down from the trees and into the barn with the others, he counted the cows a third and fourth time, making sure there was an even and accurate fifty. He also made sure the barn was bolted and locked securely.

In the morning, the sheriff did not visit Greg's ranch. After he let the cows out of the barn, he baked several plates of brownies to apologize to George Smucker, John Hansen, Sheriff Dunbar, and several members of the church. Greg made sure to count and recount his cattle each morning and evening as part of his daily routine. When his cows behaved, he rewarded them with trips to the drive-in movie theater and the occasional trough of George Smucker's homemade root beer. The happy cows thrived at his ranch. Within a couple of years, Greg brought some of his own cows to the market where he reassured his leery customers the cows were an excellent breed to raise as long as someone takes time to count them accurately.

Danny stared at Dad with his mouth open. Liz, who was working on her own homework, was equally surprised by Dad's story.

"Mommy tells us stories at bedtime, not when we are working on homework," Liz said.

The timing of Dad's story wasn't what confused Danny, it was where Dad got that story. Dad had only read them stories from their collection of children's books. Where did Dad hear such a crazy story?

"Dad," Danny said, giving him a look, "Cows don't drink root beer. They drink water and eat grass. And, they don't climb trees."

"That's not the point of the story. The point is to take the time to check your work for mistakes. If you are rushing through your homework to watch TV, you'll probably make mistakes and not learn what you need to the first time. When it comes to math, the more you fall behind, the harder it is to catch up. I don't want you to fall behind. Please, check your work more carefully. It will only take a few minutes."

"That story took more than a few minutes!" Danny protested.

"Yes, I know, but it only took a moment. That's the same kind of quick moment it will take you to correct your homework. When you're done fixing the mistakes, you may watch TV. If you need help, you know where to find me."

Losing time on listening to Dad's story and making multiple mistakes on his homework annoyed Danny. He could have been watching TV.

Looking at his homework more carefully, he realized he had confused multiplying his sevens with eights, and finished correcting all his mistakes a short while later. After Dad gave him the thumbs up, he and Liz fought over what show to watch.

The argument got them nowhere, so they gave up and decided to play instead.

Night of the

Dreamless Veggies

A story about trying new things.

Steam wavered over the bubbling pot of noodles. The diced chicken sizzled in the frying pan with the splash of olive oil, slices of bell peppers and pecans, and a sprinkling of seasoning. Dad arranged the garlic bread on the pan and placed it in the pre-heated oven.

"What are we having for dinner?" Danny asked.

"It's one of your Granny's recipes. It's one of my favorites. I thought I'd try it on you before I make it for Mom."

"What's in it?" Danny asked, crinkling up his nose.

"It's chicken, noodles, a few veggies, and a little seasoning."

"Oh," Danny said, disappointed. He hoped, for once, whipped cream and chocolate sauce were among the ingredients.

"I like noodles, but I don't like veggies," Liz grumbled from the other room.

"You should like this," Dad replied.

"Does it have sauce?" Danny asked.

"I don't like sauce, either," Liz added.

"There's no sauce. Just seasoning. Neither of you have tried this before. You haven't even given it a chance."

"Do we have to eat it?" Danny asked.

Dad looked at the bubbling and sizzling pans. He said, "Yes. This is what I'm making for dinner."

They groaned in stereo.

"Come on, kiddos. Give it a chance."

They groaned again.

"Can't we order pizza? Or, pick up fried chicken?" Danny asked. With Mom away, he had hoped Dad would be more relaxed about eating healthy.

"No. This is what we are having. Besides, you don't want to have nightmares like the family who did not eat their *vegetables, do you?" Dad asked.*

"What? What family? What vegetables? What nightmares?" Liz asked, confused.

"Oh great," Danny said. "Here we go again."

"Your mom and I offer you a variety of foods, so you can eat healthy and sample different flavors. But, the Joneses discovered there are other reasons to try new foods."

NIGHT OF THE DREAMLESS VEGGIES

The Jones family were unpacking boxes when they heard a friendly knock at the door. Mr. Jones cautiously opened the door.

"Hi there!" said Mr. Smith, a cheery, chirpy neighbor. "I'm your next door neighbor. I can see you are still unpacking. You're probably not in the mood to cook, huh?"

"We'll probably go out and grab a bite somewhere," Mrs. Jones said, joining her husband at the door.

"Nonsense! Bring yourselves over so we can properly welcome your family with a wonderful meal," the neighbor said, smiling wide.

"That's very nice, but we don't want to inconvenience you," Mr. Jones said.

"It's no trouble at all. We will expect you at six," the neighbor said.

"Thank you. That's very kind of you," Mrs. Jones said.

"Welcome to the neighborhood!"

Mr. and Mrs. Jones thanked the neighbor again and closed the door.

That night, the Jones family arrived at six o'clock. Mr. Jones managed a single knock when the door flew opened and the neighbor's wife, Mrs. Smith, welcomed the Jonses into their home. After a round of introductions, Bobby and Susie Jones played with the Smith kids, while Mr. and Mrs. Jones had a quick tour of the house. After the tour, both families sat down to the dinner table.

Mrs. Smith set a basket of freshly baked bread on the table. All the kids made yummy sounds after smelling the heavenly bread. Next, Mr. Smith lifted the roasting pan's cover with a flourish exposing the succulent chicken, glistening with its natural, greasy juices. Everyone applauded. And finally, Mrs. Smith smiled as she lifted the lid from the last pot set on the table. When the thick steam cleared, bright green vegetables glowed from within the pot. The Jones family froze.

The Joneses gave each other looks between themselves and the glowing pot of vegetables. When the pot was passed around, each of the Joneses took a small portion to be polite. It was clear that none of them wanted to be the first to try the strange, nuclear vegetable.

"Dig in!" Mr. Smith said.

The Smith family gobbled down the food, including the strange, glowing vegetable. The Jones family savored the chicken and the bread, but avoided their meager helping of the strange vegetable. While none of the neighbors were looking, Mr. Jones inspected the glowing veggie while the rest of the family watched to see if he would actually try it. He sniffed the bite on his fork, but dropped it to his plate, feigning a coughing fit.

At the end of the meal, the entire Jones family still had their untouched portions of vegetables on their plates. The neighbors didn't look insulted or disappointed, but they did look concerned.

"You don't eat vegetables?" Mr. Smith asked, giving Mrs. Smith a side glance.

"We've never seen a vegetable so…so…*green* before," Mr. Jones said.

"It's good for you to eat your greens," Mr. Smith said, chuckling nervously.

"Thank you, but no," Mrs. Jones said.

"But, you must!" Mrs. Smith said, a tad hysterical.

Mr. Jones pushed his plate away and said, "We don't have to eat it if we don't want to."

The rest of the family followed suit and also rejected the glowing veggie.

The neighbors sighed. Disappointed, Mr. Smith said, "Suit yourself."

Because the Joneses refused to eat the bizarre, luminescent vegetable, the rest of the evening was filled with awkward conversation until it was time to say, "Goodnight."

After unpacking all day and having an unusual dinner, the Jones family was ready to go to bed in their new home. Unfortunately, that night, the Jones family did not sleep well. Mr. Jones had a nightmare a giant rabbit forced him to make hundreds of paper airplanes, none of which could fly. Mrs. Jones had a nightmare that she turned into a fish and was chased by a mailman because she didn't have the correct postage. Bobby Jones had a dream about a sofa that force fed him the glowing vegetable, while Susie Jones dreamed their new house was made of chocolate, but melted from the vegetable's blinding glow. The next day, the Jones family felt tired and miserable.

They unpacked more boxes and tried to settle into their new home, but they were so tired from their lack of sleep from a nightmare-filled night, they kept unpacking boxes in the wrong rooms of the house. Bobby and Susie had completely unpacked their clothes before they realized they were in each other's rooms. They packed the clothes again, traded rooms, and started all over again. Mr. Jones had completely hooked up the entertainment center when he realized it was all set up behind the sofa. He too had to shuffle things around and start again. And, Mrs. Jones, who had thought she was putting the dishes away into the cupboard, had actually stacked up the dishes into another box instead.

A knock on the front door interrupted their confusion. It was a different neighbor. "Hello there!"

"Hi," Mr. Jones croaked, as he leaned against the doorway.

"The name's Lawson. I live just down the street. Looks like you had a rough night. Why don't you and your family come by for dinner tonight? We're having barbecue around seven o'clock."

"Sounds great. Do we need to bring anything?" Mr. Jones asked, yawning.

"Just yourselves," the neighbor said.

"Thanks," Mr. Jones mumbled, as the neighbor trotted away. Mr. Jones nodded off while standing up, until Bobby and Susie woke him up, pulled him out of the doorway, and closed the door.

The Joneses took naps before dinner, but even their afternoon naps were filled with strange nightmares. Feeling a little more refreshed after having showers, they walked down the street to the neighbor's house. The smell hit their noses from a couple houses away. The barbecue smelled delicious.

"Hello there!" Mr. Lawson said, as the family plodded into his backyard. Mrs. Lawson brought them a tray of lemonade.

When the neighbor opened the grill, glowing green smoke filled the air. Among the burger patties and hot dogs, slices of the same glowing green vegetable were grilling on the upper rack. The family looked at each other and wondered about the strange vegetable.

"Excuse me," Bobby said, "what vegetable is that?"

"This?" Mr. Lawson asked, pointing to the slices of vegetables with his barbecue tongs. "This is what they call nightlight squash. You see those trees?" he asked, pointing to willow trees growing on the edge of the yard. Bobby nodded. Many of the neighbors also had the same willow trees. Even the Joneses recalled having one or two growing in their own yard.

"Those trees are called sleeping willows. Their pollen fills the air of this neighborhood, giving people strange dreams. Some people even have nightmares. It's a ridiculous allergy, I know. Years ago, one of the neighbors discovered nightlight squash tames those strange dreams. It holds back the monsters, which is why they call it nightlight squash. That, and it has a pretty green glow."

"It is very pretty," Susie agreed.

"Whenever new neighbors arrive, many of us try to welcome them with nightlight squash," Mr. Lawson said, flipping the burgers and turning the hot dogs.

"The Smiths pushed some of that squash on us last night," Mr. Jones said.

"But, they never told us why to eat it," Bobby said.

"I've never cared much for squash," Mr. Jones said, crinkling up his nose at the slices sizzling on the grill.

"I know it's not for everyone, but having some now and then helps ease the dreams. Now, who wants a burger and who wants a dog?"

Both kids took hot dogs and a bit of the grilled nightlight squash. Both Mr. And Mrs. Jones took burgers, but refused the nightlight squash.

That night, the kids slept peacefully. They never woke once in the night and felt very refreshed in the morning. Their parents, on the other hand, had another night filled with stranger, crazier dreams. Mrs. Jones had recurring dreams of climbing up the sleeping willows and falling. She even fell out of the bed—*twice*! Mr. Jones had recurring dreams of fighting off an octopus that tried to force feed him the nightlight squash. In the morning, he spent several minutes untangling himself from the bed sheets wrapped around his arms and legs.

The following day, the kids had completely unpacked and arranged their rooms the way they liked well before lunchtime. They went outside, made new friends of the other neighbor kids, and played hide and seek for a majority of the day. Mr. and Mrs. Jones still had issues unpacking, but did not get very far because they kept falling asleep. They woke up when the other would scream at more scary dreams.

Late in the afternoon, the kids came inside with a plate of bright green muffins made with nightlight squash. The muffins were a welcome gift from yet another neighbor. Mrs. Jones, who had slept and screamed through lunchtime, was starving and ate one of the delicious muffins. Mr. Jones still didn't trust the strange vegetable and fixed himself a sandwich, which was only bread and mustard, because in his dazed condition, he put the cheese and lunchmeat on an oven mitt instead between slices of bread.

At night, the kids and their mom slept soundly. Mr. Jones had another recurring nightmare of the neighbors trying to poison him with bubbling potions that glowed bright green. He tried to yell for help, which came out as a stifled moan. Mrs. Jones slept right through her husband's outbursts and snored at him from her deep, peaceful sleep.

The following day, Mrs. Jones finished unpacking everything, except Mr. Jones's boxes for his desk and a few of his collectibles. He was so tired, he was completely useless in helping unpack and settle into their new home. The family couldn't help but laugh when he fell asleep, hunched over, into a large cardboard box. When he sprang out of the box screaming, they thought he looked like a poorly made Jack-in-the-box.

That evening, Mrs. Jones chopped up some nightlight squash and blended it into one of her husband's favorite dishes. Mrs. Jones and the kids ate some more of the squash, but Mr. Jones sat and stared at the meager portion scooped onto his plate.

"What if I don't like it?" Mr. Jones asked.

"It's good for you," Mrs. Jones said.

"It'll help you sleep better at night," Bobby said.

"No more bad dreams," Susie added.

Mr. Jones made a face at the glowing green bits of his meal. He frowned and said, "I know I'm not going to like it, and it's going to ruin one of my favorite meals."

"I've only added it just this one time. Try a couple of bites and tell me what you think," his wife said.

Mr. Jones speared a bit onto his fork. He closed his eyes and stuck out his tongue. The moment the food touched his tongue, he started making gagging noises. His head drooped forward. The family thought maybe he was having an allergic reaction to the squash, but he had actually fallen asleep. His face fell directly into his mashed potatoes.

Mrs. Jones woke him gently and helped wipe gravy and potatoes off his face. She encouraged him to take one good-sized bite. Mr. Jones considered the previous taste of the squash he had before he fell asleep in his food. He decided it wasn't his favorite vegetable, but not nearly as bad as he had expected. He had three good-sized bites, which satisfied the rest of his family. He still didn't care too much for the taste and washed it down with a large glass of milk.

That night, everyone had a peaceful night's sleep in their new home and everyone felt wonderful in the morning. From that moment on, they didn't have the nightlight squash with every meal, but would fix it sometimes before the nightmares returned. They learned the importance of trying new foods, especially ones that shine a light on bad dreams.

"Daddy," Liz said, and put her hand on his arm. "You are telling the story wrong."

"What's wrong with how I told the story? Dad asked.

"Stories are for bedtime, not dinnertime."

"Anytime can be storytime," Dad said.

"No, Daddy. Besides," Liz said, tilting her head and giving her dad one of her looks, "That stuff could never happen."

"Maybe. Maybe not. Look," Dad said, "I shared that story with you, because it is important to try new things. It's not like it is completely new and strange. I know you two like noodles and chicken and do not like sauce, that's why I thought I would try it. It's one of my favorites and I'd like your honest opinion. Do you think Mom would like it?"

Danny and Liz eyed the food on their plates cautiously.

"Three bites?" Danny asked.

"I'm not negotiating with you, Danny. This is what's for dinner."

Danny folded his arms and stared at the food on his plate. He liked chicken and he liked noodles. What kid didn't? The cooked slices of bell peppers and chunks of pecans are what made it unappetizing for him. He would have the same reaction if someone dared offer him a hamburger with mayonnaise.

Liz put a tiny morsel on her fork and popped it quickly into her mouth. She chewed it and nodded, "Not bad, Dad." She scooped a larger bite into her mouth, including the bell peppers and pecans. "It's good. Mommy will love this."

That settled it. If his younger sister could eat it, so could he. With much hesitation, Danny finally tried a bite. "Yeah. I guess Mom'll like this." Although he never admitted liking the meal himself, the evidence of missing chicken, noodles and *pecans from his plate proved that he at least tolerated most of the meal's ingredients.*

The Kite of Jealousy

A story about sharing and cooperation.

After dinner, Dad worked at his computer. Danny knew his dad did Quality Assurance. Danny had a good laugh when Liz misheard it as Quilting Insurance and thought he sold insurance policies for blankets and comforters. When Dad explained he tested and tried to break software. Danny wondered, if something worked, why try to break it? Dad said it makes the software better. Dad joked about wanting to break more things for work before relaxing for the evening. As he typed, Danny and Liz went to the playroom. A familiar argument soon erupted, breaking his concentration.

"Give it back!" Liz yelled.

"You said I could play with it!" Danny said.

"That was yesterday! I want it back!"

"Stop it! Go away!"

Yesterday, Danny had found a plastic figurine from a cartoon movie neither of them had ever watched. Liz got the toy months ago from a fast food kid's meal. Mom had taken Liz to lunch after a doctor's appointment. Liz had played with the toy no more than three days after getting it, and had ignored it since. Liz gave Danny permission to play with it over the weekend, but since Mom had left for her trip, she desperately wanted it back.

The same argument happened all the time. One child rediscovered something neither had any interest in for a long time. The moment one showed the slightest interest, both coveted it as the most fascinating object in the world.

"But, it's mine!" Liz said.

"Hey kiddos," Dad said from downstairs.

"I'll give it back later!" Danny yelled, as the cyclical fight raged on.

"Hey kiddos!" Dad said louder.

"Let go!" Liz yelled, trying to tug it free of her brother's *tight grip.*

"Leave me alone!" Danny yelled, escalating the feud.

"Daniel! Elizabeth! Here! Now!"

"Now you've done it," Danny grumbled.

The kids approached Dad at his desk, both tugging at a little, plastic toy.

"Is that what you're fighting over?" Dad asked, pointing at the toy.

They both yelled their arguments of why they deserved the toy more. Dad held up his hands to stop them.

Dad asked, "How do you think the toy feels about this argument?"

Danny looked at his Dad like his brain was broken. Liz looked confused.

"Let me tell you the story about two kids and a kite."

They both groaned.

"Not another story," Danny moaned.

"Not this much before bedtime," Liz protested.

THE KITE OF JEALOUSY

Once upon a time, a brother and sister lived in a very boring little town that was so dull and boring, the place was just called Town. Everyone lived very dull, slow lives in Town. They preferred doing the same things over and over, day after day. Even the clouds floating across the sky above Town were too blobby and dull to resemble anything exciting. In fact, the most exciting cloud to ever pass over Town almost looked like a filing cabinet.

The brother and sister lived with their mother and father in a tan house that looked a lot like the other houses in Town. They ate bland foods and wore clothes similar to all their friends. Neither child owned a toy to call their own. It's not that their parents didn't approve of toys, nor that toys were outlawed or illegal. The stores in Town didn't sell many toys or games. Other stores in other cities sold toys and games, which were much too exciting for the people of Town.

One day, the brother and sister walked home from school, like they did every day. The sister looked up and saw a lime-green, diamond-shaped kite stuck in a tree by the playground. Her brother paid more attention to the rock he kicked down the sidewalk and did not see the kite. Since school had let out and the afternoon was still young, no other children were around to claim ownership of the kite stuck in the tree. The sister tugged on her brother's sleeve and pointed at the kite. He climbed the tree and untangled the kite, its tail, and the string from the tree branches. Once free of the tree, he glided the kite down to his sister waiting below.

When they got home, they repaired the kite with some of their old homework, a bit of beige tape, and an off-white ribbon. They used bits of string the brother had collected from the newspaper stand near the community center. He had collected so much, his ball of string was almost the size of a volleyball.

Since the sister had spotted the kite in the tree, she flew the repaired kite first. Every few minutes, they traded turns flying the kite. Sharing their first kite was one of the most enjoyable experiences they had ever known. The wind was perfect. They flew it until sunset, when it was time to go home.

The brother and sister shared a room. They hung the kite on their closet door, which was the perfect spot for both of them to see it from their beds.

In the middle of the night, as the children slept, the kite whispered to the sister, "You found me stuck in the tree. If it wasn't for you, I would still be there. You are my favorite. Tomorrow, you should fly me all by yourself." This made the sister smile in her sleep.

The next day, after school, the sister rushed home to get the kite to fly it. The brother, who had a book report due the next day, was jealous his sister flew the kite by herself. She let out some string to allow the kite to go higher while her brother read his book under a nearby tree. He wished he could fly it, but knew he had to finish reading his book first.

The wind slowed and the kite crashed to the ground. The boy leapt to his feet, worried the kite might be damaged. He dropped his book and rushed to the kite. Luckily, the kite was still in good condition. As the brother looked over the kite, it whispered to him, "You climbed the tree and rescued me. If it wasn't for you and your ball of string, I would not be able to fly. You are my favorite. You should take a break from reading that book and fly me all by yourself."

"It's my turn," the brother declared and began to fly the kite.

"I thought you had a book to read," the sister said.

He ignored her and helped the kite soar higher into the air.

The kite whispered to the sister, "Today is your day to fly me. Take the string from him."

The sister grabbed at the string and said, "You should be reading. I want to fly the kite!"

The kite whispered to the brother, "Do not let her take me away from you. Let out more string."

The brother pulled the string away from his sister and let out more.

As the kite sailed higher, the fight between the siblings escalated. The kite continued to tell the sister to try to take the string from her brother, and told the brother to fly it further and further from her reach. Up and up went the kite where the wind blew strong. The ball of string shrank and the line curved high up into the air to a tiny, green speck that was the kite. Their argument grew louder as the kite flew higher until—SNAP!—the string broke!

The string tumbled to the ground in a long wavy line across the park and neighboring houses. The kite, a small dot twirling in the sky, flew away. As it drifted higher and further from the brother and sister far below, they never heard the kite say, "You are a mighty wind. Without you, I could not fly. You are my favorite. Now, I can fly without string tying me down."

The kite flew far, far away. Neither the brother nor the sister ever played with the kite again, but they still had each other. From that moment on, the brother and sister never let any object come between their friendship.

"See? Don't let a toy come between you two," Dad said.

"Kites don't have mouths. How could it talk?" Liz asked, confused.

"It's just a stupid story," Danny said, rolling his eyes.

"I'm just saying you two should either take turns playing with that, find a game where you both can play with it, or one of you find something else to play with."

"Come on, Lizzie," Danny said.

The two decided to play Chutes 'n Ladders using the toy as an Extra Move Trophy. Whoever had the toy could either take another turn or use it to move one more space to avoid the chutes. When they used the toy for an extra move, they had to give it to the other player. Danny let Liz have the toy first. As they played, they pretended the toy acted like the kite from the story, cheering on the player who possessed it.

After Danny won, they put away the board game in the cabinet, while the toy remained, neglected once again, on the kitchen table.

The Shelf Live of Berries

A story about procrastination.

At bedtime, the kids asked to be tucked in. The Tuck-In had become hit or miss in the evenings, especially with Danny. At times, he wanted to play quietly in his room until he felt tired. With Mom out of town, both he and Liz wanted the comfort of the old bedtime ritual.

For Liz, she liked how her parents could flip the sheet out and over the mattress as if making the bed, except she would lie in the middle of the bed while they did this. The sheet would gently settle, completely covering her. Then, Mom or Dad would pull the sheet, revealing Liz's head. She would giggle and ask for them to do it all over again. If Danny remembered correctly, seven was the high score for the number of times either of their parents would do this before calling it quits.

Danny, on the other hand, always liked when Dad tucked the sheet and blanket tight so he could pretend to be an escape artist. Danny would say he didn't want Dad tickling him, but really, he didn't mind it. Danny thought it added to the escape artist experience. For Danny, escape artistry was tiring work, and he could stand no more than two attempts.

Dad tucked in Liz first. Then, tucked Danny in tight, like a big burrito.

As Danny successfully escaped the sheets, he said, "I miss Mom."

"I do, too,"

"Me too!" Liz called from the other room.

"She wasn't here to help me study for my science test," Danny said.

"What about me? I could have helped you," Dad said. "Did you do any studying?"

"Well," he said, and cowered under the sheets, wishing he could escape the conversation.

"Daniel," Dad said, his voice sounding stern and

disappointed.

"A little bit?" he squeaked.

Dad smirked with disbelief. With the stink he raised about his math homework, he didn't blame Dad for not believing him. The teacher did go over what was going to be on the test in class. Didn't that count?

"If you have a test tomorrow, you should have studied. And, if you needed help, you should have asked me."

"But, Mom..."

"No. Don't blame Mom. She's not here right now. Besides, studying for the test is your responsibility, not Mom's. Why didn't you study earlier?"

"I forgot?" he squeaked, again.

Dad gave him another look.

"Ok. I thought about studying a little, but when I finished my homework, I wanted to watch TV, and then there was dinner, and then Liz and I were playing..."

"It sounds like you were procrastinating."

"What's that?"

"Procrastinating? It means to delay doing something. Want to hear another story?"

"Another story?" Danny groaned. If a story was his only punishment, Danny sighed, "I guess. Does it have crazy cows or talking kites in it?"

"No, this one is about a baker and some special berries."

"Do the berries talk?"

"No, but the berries taught the baker an important lesson why she should not procrastinate."

THE SHELF LIFE OF BERRIES

There once was a baker named Tabitha who was well known for her cakes, cookies, brownies, and all sorts of treats, none of them good for you, but all the most delicious-tasting sweets anyone ever tasted. Because of her fame for her desserts and treats, her baking services were in high demand. She did her best to please all her customers, even the more difficult ones. Her most difficult customer, Wilhelmina Snute, was always very picky. For Tabitha, Ms. Snute's demands took the fun out of baking.

One Saturday morning, Wilhelmina Snute bustled into Tabitha's bakery, immediately issuing demands. She ignored the other customers, oblivious of Tabitha already working on the morning's orders. Ms. Snute slapped a piece of paper on the counter, and blurted, "My dear, I'm in a dreadful hurry, but I need you to call this farmer. He simply grows the most delicious Dracon berries. I need you to purchase some of these berries and bake me something, I don't care what it is, but it must be something unique, scrumptious, and full of Dracon berries. It must be done by Friday. Those berries won't last, you know. Thank you, dear! Ta ta!"

Wilhelmina Snute bustled out the door again.

Tabitha picked up the slip of paper, crumpled it in her fist, and growled, "Oh, that Ms. Snute."

She shoved the farmer's phone number into her pocket, and continued her work. Ms. Snute could wait.

When things slowed down, the local farmer stopped by to make his usual Saturday delivery. Tabitha bought her fruits and vegetables from his local garden.

Tabitha asked him, "Do you have Dracon berries?"

"I wish," he said, "Those berries are delicious, but temperamental. I know the guy who grows them. I'll see him Monday. If you'd like, I can bring you some. Mind you, you've got to be quick. They'll only last about five days."

Tabitha paid the farmer for her usual delivery, and a little extra to bring her some of the Dracon berries. She no longer had to call Ms. Snute's farmer. Now, she needed to think up a unique recipe. But, Ms. Snute could wait. The weekend was full of other things to do, like baking cakes for birthdays and weddings, not to mention the Sunday breakfast breads for the local churches.

On Monday, Tabitha looked through her cookbooks for the perfect recipe to use for Ms. Snute's Dracon berries. Muffins were good, but not unique enough. She considered baking a pie, but pies used too many berries. If she had to buy Dracon berries for Ms. Snute, she wanted to make something special enough to share with as many of her other customers as possible.

Around midday, the farmer delivered two cartons of Dracon berries. Tabitha tasted a single berry, and had to admit, the berries were very delicious. She had the berries, but didn't have a recipe. She would think of one later. Ms. Snute could wait.

A jingling sound rang through the town. The ice cream man was coming! Every week, she and the ice cream man had a tradition. She baked a large batch of fresh out-of-the-oven cookies and he churned fresh homemade ice cream. Each Monday, they hosted the afternoon's Ice Cream Sandwich Social in the village square outside her shop. She couldn't refuse a weekly tradition, not when everyone expected it. Thinking up a new recipe could wait until the next day.

On Tuesday, Tabitha arrived in her shop early. She wanted to think of a new recipe, but she daydreamed about cookies from the day before. The new recipe could wait. Besides, she had a customer.

A gentleman wearing the fanciest clothes the baker had ever seen burst into the bakery. He was the butler for Lady Penelope Von VanDerShnork, the richest woman in town.

"Lady Penelope is hosting the royal family from the Island of Gallafanook."

"Where is the Island of Gallafanook?" Tabitha asked.

"I expect somewhere surrounded by a lot of water, but that's not important. The royal family has never tried waffles. Lady Penelope is in urgent need of waffles!" the butler said.

Tabitha looked at her two cartons of berries and thought of the recipe she had yet to invent. She said, "Don't worry, sir. I will prepare Lady Penelope plenty of delicious waffles for her and her guests."

She loaded up some supplies in the limousine waiting outside and traveled with the butler to Lady Penelope's mansion, where Tabitha made a fresh batch of her finest waffles dusted with a bit of powdered sugar. As an extra special treat, she used the Dracon berries to make a delicious syrup to pour over the waffles. Lady Penelope and her guests were extremely pleased with the waffles, and especially the syrup.

When Tabitha returned to her bakery, she called the farmer to order more Dracon berries. He said he would bring her some more in the morning. Ms. Snute and a new recipe would have to wait until tomorrow.

On Wednesday, the farmer brought Tabitha another couple cartons of the delicious berries. She tried to think of a recipe, but she daydreamed about filling each waffle square with the berry syrup.

She looked out the window and the sunlight seemed strange and not quite right. The baker stepped outside to see what was happening. One of her neighbors said there was going to be a total eclipse and everyone was heading down to the park to watch it through pinhole cameras and celebrate the event. The eclipse had already started, which is why the light outside seemed so strange.

Tabitha wanted to finally figure out a recipe, but a solar eclipse, especially a *total* solar eclipse was *very* rare. How many times in her life would she get to see one of those? Ms. Snute could wait.

Tabitha decided to lock up her shop for the day, head down to the park, and celebrate with the rest of the town. Thousands of people gathered to celebrate the event. She could not resist the special karaoke for people to get up on stage and sing about the sun, moon, or other songs of space. She took lessons on how to moonwalk, and the children in town encouraged her to jump in the bouncy castle. Tabitha helped the astronomy club make and sell moon pies at a booth to raise money.

When the eclipse ended, she returned to her shop. It was late in the afternoon and she was exhausted from all the singing, dancing, and bouncing, not to mention helping make several moon pies for the astronomy club. She decided to go home and rest. Tomorrow was another day. Ms. Snute could wait.

On Thursday, Tabitha opened her shop late. She still felt a bit tired from the previous day's celebration and slept in a little bit. Cookies and syrup and moon pies danced in her mind. An idea for a new recipe was forming, but disappeared when her first customer of the day arrived.

Mrs. Pennyworth from the Society of Women Proficient in Gaming had arrived with an emergency order of little cakes for the annual bridge tournament to be held that evening at the convention center. Tabitha always found it amusing the acronym for Mrs. Pennyworth's organization spelled out SOW-PIG, but was not amused to bake such a large order of cakes on demand with such short notice. Since SOW-PIG was a well-known group in the community, she agreed to take the order. Hopefully, the idea for her new recipe would come back to her. For now, Ms. Snute could wait. SOW-PIG needed her.

She baked an assortment of little cakes for the tournament in various flavors, including chocolate, orange-creme, mint, and strawberry. The order was so large, it took most of Tabitha's flour, sugar, and eggs to complete. She and the delivery boy delivered the hundreds of little cakes to the convention center, and arranged them on the dessert table to look like different playing cards. Even her petite cakes had tiny fondant clubs, diamonds, spades, and hearts.

On the way back to the bakery, she stopped by the superstore to refill her ingredients. An old man ahead of her in line took an extra long time by paying for his items with an assortment of coins from a very large jar. By the time she returned to the bakery to unloaded the flour, sugar, and eggs, the sun had set. After baking and decorating hundreds of little cakes and shopping at the super store, she felt exhausted. It had been a very long day. A new recipe for Ms. Snute could wait a little longer.

At night, lying in bed, dancing treats filled her mind. Cookies. Syrup. Moon pies. And now, tiny cakes. She knew her imagination was trying to tell her something. If she made something small, like the tiny cakes, she could share it with lots of people. Cookies were a small treat she could share with many people. What kind of cookies had berries? Oatmeal cookies sometimes had raisins or dried cranberries, but that wouldn't be very unique. Would a Dracon berry cookie be unique? What if she combined a cookie recipe with a pie recipe? A little cookie with a little bit of pie filling in the center. The Dracon berries would be perfect for her new cookie-pie recipe. She couldn't wait to try her new recipe in the morning.

Friday morning, a well-rested Tabitha arrived at her bakery, ready to bake her cookie-pies, but...

A school bus full of third-graders arrived for a field trip. She had already planned to teach them how to bake cookies. What luck! They could help her try her special new recipe!

"Instead of making chocolate chip cookies, like I originally planned," she said, "I thought you could help me with a *new* recipe! Cookie-pies!"

"No! We want chocolate chip cookies!" the kids demanded.

"Not cookie-pies?"

The kids chanted, "Chocolate chip! Chocolate chip! Chocolate chip!"

Tabitha sighed and gave in. She had promised the kids chocolate chip cookies. Ms. Snute's cookie-pies would need to wait one more day.

The kids learned how to make chocolate chip cookies, and had the best field trip ever! The teachers and chaperones were curious about the cookie-pies. She described them and the grown ups thought they sounded delicious. One of the teachers had tried the special berries and knew how delicious they were. They could not wait.

"I have put it off long enough. I will definitely make them tomorrow," Tabitha said.

On Saturday morning, when Tabitha entered her bakery, she smelled something horrible. She wondered if an animal, like a squirrel, or a raccoon, or maybe even a skunk had broken into her kitchen at night and died. She was sad to discover, the smell wasn't a dead squirrel, raccoon, or skunk, but her cartons of berries. Overnight, the berries had all spoiled and stunk up her kitchen. She threw away all the cartons of spoiled berries and throughly cleaned her kitchen instead.

The teachers and chaperones from the field trip arrived to try the cookie-pies, but couldn't stand the stink coming from the kitchen. They were disappointed there would be no cookie-pies at this time.

When the farmer arrived with the week's delivery of fruits and vegetables, he and Tabitha could still smell the odor of the putrid berries in the kitchen.

"I did tell you the berries are only good for five days. If you don't eat or cook with them within the first five days, they tend to spoil very quickly," said the farmer.

"I know. I can smell," Tabitha said, sadly, "I should have used them sooner instead of setting it aside for so many other things."

Since Dracon berries were no longer in season and any remaining ones smelled too horrible to go near, Tabitha baked a batch of blueberry cookie-pies for Wilhelmina Snute and apologized for taking too long to find and bake her something with the Dracon berries. Ms. Snute appreciated the uniqueness of the cookie-pies.

One year later, Tabitha was more prepared. She dug out her cookie-pie recipe and scheduled time to bake them, regardless of any other distractions. She even contacted the farmer the day before the Dracon berries went on sale so she could be one of the first to buy them. When she bought them and used them to make cookie-pies, her customers thought she had created the best treat they had ever tasted. She had learned her lesson by preparing ahead of time and staying focused instead of procrastinating.

"So, you're saying I shouldn't have let TV or dinner or playing with Liz distract me from studying earlier?" Danny asked.

"Yes. Well, not dinner. You need to eat, too. You could have studied before watching TV or playing with Liz. Unless you have a time machine, you can't go back in time to study when you should have," Dad said.

"What am I supposed to do now? You're telling me I should study, but you're also telling me to go to bed!" Danny said, his voice rising.

"Calm down. It is bedtime, but if you want, I won't be upset if you stay up a little bit to study right now. In the morning, maybe you can look over your science notes at breakfast. If there's time, maybe I can help quiz you."

Danny agreed his Dad had a good idea. He would skim through his science book instead of reading comics before bed.

As his Dad left to check on Liz, Danny said, "Hey, Dad?"

"Yes?"

"In that story, the baker put off baking the cookies, but it gave her time to think up a new recipe. So, is practiceacation a good thing?"

"The word is procrastination. I know. Big word. And yes, you are right. It can be a good thing, especially when you need time to think about something for a while. The problem is when there is a time limit. She ran out of time, kind of like you running low on time to study for your science test."

"I'll go get my book. I'll look it over again in the morning, too."

"Sounds good. I'll leave you alone, so I'm not distracting you. Relax, study some, get some sleep. When it's time to take your test, just try your best. And, next time you know there will be a test, hopefully you'll prepare for it better ahead of time.

Okay?"

"Okay." *Danny climbed out of bed to get his school bag and said,* "Thanks, Dad. Goodnight."

"Goodnight, Danny."

The Cover Up

A story about admitting to mistakes.

Tuesday, after school, Danny and Liz gave a sigh of relief when Dad picked them up on time.

In the back seat, Liz hugged her backpack. She unzipped it and peeked inside. Her backpack contained something that was not hers. Worse than that, what was not hers broke earlier in the day.

"You have looked in your backpack about a million times. Even while waiting for Dad, you did that. What have you got in there?" Danny said.

Liz wished her brother would be quiet. Dad glanced at her in the rearview mirror, but when their eyes met, she quickly looked out the window. Worrying about what to do, she looked into her backpack again, as if it would tell her the answers.

"What's in there? Is it a turtle? If so, I want to see it," Danny said.

"Mind your own business. It's not a turtle," Liz mumbled. She zipped her backpack closed again.

"Weirdo," Danny said.

"You're the weirdo. Why would I have a turtle?" Liz asked.

Danny shrugged. He rolled his eyes at her and then gazed out the window.

At home, Liz got out her homework and then quickly zipped her pack closed again. She didn't want her nosy brother finding the broken figurine. She didn't know how to fix it. The best plan she could think of would be to sneak it back onto the shelf while nobody was looking. Maybe when someone finds it, they'll figure it broke falling off the shelf.

Liz took her time on her homework. It was pretty easy, but she read it over again and again, and even erased and rewrote part of it to buy her some time. Danny finished his homework quickly, and finally went into the other room to watch TV.

"You doing okay on your homework? Need any help?" Dad

asked from his desk.

"Nope. Just finishing it up now," Liz said.

As she put away her homework, Liz pulled out the two pieces of a wooden figurine of the Caterpillar from Alice in Wonderland. The base of the mushroom broke off from the cap, but the Caterpillar and his hookah were still attached to the top. The Caterpillar's mushroom was one of Mom's figurines. Ellie adored Alice in Wonderland and had collected various figurines and knickknacks depicting different elements from the books. Knowing Mom favorited the Cheshire Cat, Liz took the Caterpillar to show her teacher, who had been reading bits of the book to the class. The mushroom survived the teacher asking her to pass it around for all the kids to see, but when she took it out again later to show her friends, Liz dropped it and it broke. She felt horrible. She had not asked for permission to borrow it. The figurine was Mom's, who was out of town. She decided to take it to school anyway, and deeply regretted her decision.

Liz snuck the mushroom back onto the shelf with the other Alice in Wonderland figures. She carefully balanced the cap on top of the base, then quickly walked away to join her brother.

As they watched TV, she heard a soft "clunk" from the shelf. Dad got up from his desk to investigate. Liz forced herself not to look at Dad or the shelf, and concentrated on the TV. A moment later, Dad entered the room and cleared his throat.

"Liz, what happened to Mom's Caterpillar mushroom?" Dad asked, holding the two pieces.

"I don't know. What mushroom?" Liz asked, her eyes glued to the TV.

"Liz, look at me. What happened to the Caterpillar mushroom?"

Liz glanced at the pieces in Dad's hands, but did not make eye contact. "Looks like it broke," she said, and then stared at the TV.

"Do you have any idea how it broke?" Dad asked.

"No. I don't know. Maybe it just broke," she said.

"I'm having a hard time believing your story that it 'just broke'. Unless the way the universe works has changed, things usually don't spontaneously break. They might wear down over time, but this is not that old. Most of the time, there is a reason for something breaking. If there is a reason, I'd prefer you tell me. Liz, what have we told you?"

"The cover up is worse than the crime," Liz mumbled.

"That's right. When you hide from the truth, you aren't fixing the problem. You are avoiding fixing the mistake. I know a story about a zookeeper who made a serious mistake and tried to hide it from others."

"Ha ha. You have to listen to one of Dad's crazy stories," Danny teased.

Dad warned Danny with a glance. Danny chuckled nervously and returned to watching TV.

"Let's go sit in the other room, so we don't disturb your brother," Dad said.

Liz followed Dad to the dining room. They each took a seat at the dining table. Dad set the two pieces of the figurine between them. Liz slouched in her chair, bracing herself for another one of Dad's crazy stories.

THE COVER UP

There once was a new zookeeper at the city zoo. Fresh out of college after earning his degree in Animal Science, he felt confident in his abilities to take good care of all the animals.

The zoo had a few older keepers who had worked at this zoo for many years. The new keeper was eager to show off his skills to impress his coworkers.

"I'm sure you'll do just fine," said one of the senior zookeepers. "Just watch out for the lion."

"How hard can a lion be?" the new keeper asked. "I got all A's in my Lion Studies class. They don't sound any more difficult than any of the other animals."

The senior keepers laughed. One of them said, "Oh, you'll need to use extra care with our lion."

"Yeah, this zoo's lion will trick you if you're not careful," said another senior keeper.

The new keeper thought the others were teasing him since he was the new guy.

Still confident of his knowledge of lions, the new keeper approached the lion's cage at feeding time. The new keeper looked at the lion lounging on a large, flat rock under the midday sun. It did not seem any different than the ones he had read about.

Lying on its back, the lion opened his lazy eyes. He rolled over onto his stomach to get a better look at the new zookeeper. He crouched low and twitched his tail as the new zookeeper went about his business. A thought popped into the lion's head. His mouth curled into a wicked grin.

After the new zookeeper put the lion in the holding area so he could clean the main habitat, the lion used a claw to pick the lock and escape from the holding area. Once free, the lion walked through the zoo on its hind legs, pretending to be a person in a lion costume. He waved at the children and stopped to take pictures with families on his way to the zoo's exit. By the time the new keeper finished preparing the lion's habitat, the lion had successfully escaped the zoo.

The new keeper felt deeply embarrassed about his mistake. How could he tell the other keepers what happened when they warned him about the lion? What if they found out the lion escaped the zoo? Everyone would panic! He might even be fired on his first day at work! What was he going to do?

This is what he did. The new keeper found a yellow raincoat from the lost and found, a bit of frayed rope, and a yellow highlighter to color the strings of a frizzy mop. Together, these things made a not perfect, but passable lion costume. He put on his lion costume, crawled around the habitat and roared as loud as he could. As he pretended to be a lion, he thought about how he might catch the real lion and bring it back.

Meanwhile…Since it was feeding time, the lion found an all-you-can-eat Chinese buffet in town and stuffed himself with as many egg rolls and as much Kung Pao Chicken as he could eat.

Back at the zoo, the new keeper saw the other keepers walking around asking people if they had seen the new guy. The new keeper realized he couldn't stay dressed up as a lion forever—especially if he needed to go out and find the real lion. Besides, as much as he liked lions, he didn't like pretending to be one. He figured he must be doing a good job pretending to be a lion since many people took pictures and applauded when he roared.

The new keeper had another idea. While nobody was looking he took the sloth out of its habitat, dressed it up in the lion costume, and placed it in the lion habitat. Then, to replace the sloth, he took one of the stuffed animal sloths from the gift shop and taped it to the tree in the sloth's habitat. Now, he could go out and find the real lion.

Meanwhile…The manager told the lion to leave the Chinese restaurant since the buffet was completely out of food. When all the food is gone, that is all anyone can eat. Happy and stuffed, the lion decided he needed a nap. He walked down the street to the nearest furniture store to find a comfy bed.

Back at the zoo, the new keeper almost made it to the exit before he was stopped by one of the zoo's visitors. A teacher taking her class on a field trip asked, "Do you work here?"

"Yes, I do," said the new keeper.

"Good. You should know that some of the kids are concerned about your animals. They tell me the lion is moving in slow motion and the sloth fell out of its tree and rolled under a bush. You might want to check on them."

"Thank you for letting me know," the new keeper said.

The new keeper had another idea. He put roller skates on the sloth dressed in the lion costume. Then, he gave one of the monkeys a banana and told it to push the sloth around the lion habitat. He then sewed some velcro onto the stuffed animal sloth's hands and feet to help it stay on the tree branch. With the fake lion in motion and the stuffed animal sloth secured, he headed toward the exit to find the missing lion.

Meanwhile…The manager asked the lion to leave the furniture store. During a really good stretch, the lion's claws accidentally popped the waterbed he slept on and flooded part of the store. Sopping wet, the lion went to another store down the street to find a fresh set of towels.

Back at the zoo, a father and his two kids stopped the new keeper before he could reach the exit.

"What kind of zoo are you running here?" the father said. "Somehow, a monkey got into the lion's cage and is chasing that poor lion around! What kind of zoo has a lion afraid of monkeys?!"

The father was so outraged, he took his kids' hands and stormed out of the zoo.

"Hey, new guy," said one of the other keepers. "The sloth isn't eating and refuses to get out of his tree. See if you can do something about that, will ya?"

The new keeper turned around and went to fix the problems with the fake lion and the stuffed-animal sloth.

Meanwhile...The lion found some clean towels at a department store to dry himself off. The towels made his mane extra frizzy, sticking out in all directions. The manager asked the lion to leave the store, and told the lion to stop scaring the children. Before leaving the store, the lion looked in the mirror to see for himself. He did look like something had frightened him. He thought it was funny— anything that could scare a lion that much must be *really* scary. The lion walked down the street, scaring more children, and looked for a hairdresser to fix his mane.

Back at the zoo, the new keeper took the costume off the sloth and returned the sloth to its habitat. He swapped out the stuffed animal sloth for a wooden rocking horse which was painted to look like a zebra. As the new keeper dressed the rocking zebra in the lion costume, the real lion strolled into his habitat sporting a nice haircut and a belly full of Chinese food.

"What are you doing, new guy?" the lion asked.

The new keeper explained how he tried to cover up the missing lion by using the costume he made. He explained the sloth and the monkey. He explained how he used the roller skates, the stuffed animal, and the rocking zebra. He explained how he spent all day covering up the fact the lion had escaped, he had no time to look for the lion, but was glad the lion finally returned to his cage.

The lion said, "Which is better? On the one paw, you admit to making a mistake, telling the other zookeepers that I got out, and then you and the other keepers meet me for lunch at the Chinese buffet. On the other paw, you did all that crazy stuff to cover up your mistake, and you didn't even have time to look for me. And, you know, once the other keepers find out they missed out on Chinese buffet, they are going to be upset with you. Plus, the people working in the gift shop are going to be mad at you for using the toys without permission. You might even be fired after your first day on the job! So, I ask you again, which is better?"

"You're right, lion," the new keeper said sadly. "I should have admitted my mistake."

"The cover up is always worse than the crime, my friend," the lion said, patting the new keeper on the shoulder with his large paw. "Now, get out of my cage."

"See? If you go out of your way to hide the truth, it's just going to make things worse for you."

"Are you going to fire me?" she croaked.

"No," Dad said.

"Are you going to punish me?"

"Maybe. Why did you try to cover it up?"

"Because, I didn't want to get in trouble."

Dad nodded, "The truth has ways of revealing itself, just like the mushroom falling apart. Do you want to tell me what really happened to it?"

Liz sighed. Tears welled up in her eyes, and she mumbled, "I borrowed Mommy's Caterpillar mushroom without asking. She wasn't here for me to ask her. I wanted to show my teacher and friends. When I showed it to Molly, I dropped it and it broke."

"See? You told me the truth. Turns out it was an accident. Was that so bad?" Dad asked.

"No," Liz said, sniffling. "I didn't know how to tell you. I thought you'd be mad at me. And, Mom is going to be really mad when she finds out."

"Do I sound mad?" Dad asked.

"Not really."

"I'm not mad, but I am disappointed. Thank you for telling me what happened."

Dad gave Liz a big hug. Liz mumbled into Dad's shoulder, "I miss Mommy."

"I miss her, too. Is that why you brought the mushroom? To remind you of Mom?"

Liz nodded.

"Why don't you watch some TV with Danny. I'm going find the wood glue. You can help me put it back together. Ok?"

"Ok. Thanks, Daddy."

Dad went to the garage to fetch the wood glue. When he returned, Liz helped him fix the broken figurine. He dabbed a bit of glue to the base of the mushroom and Liz placed the cap on top. Some of the glue squished out from between the two parts, but at least it would hold. Liz hoped it would stay together until Mom came back. She dreaded telling Mom about the broken mushroom, but Dad assured her that telling Mom was the right thing to do.

Three Big Wishes

A story about too much of a good thing.

Liz asked Dad what was for dinner, but she and Danny paid more attention to the cartoons than Dad's response. In the back of her mind, Liz registered Dad might have repeated what was for dinner, or may have asked them what they wanted for dinner. It was hard to tell. The cartoon was so funny, she and Danny belly laughed while Dad talked to them.

Standing between the kids and the TV to force their attention on him, Dad announced, "As I said, because you tried something new for dinner last night, I thought I'd make you a special treat tonight. For dinner, we're having waffles!"

"Waffles? Really? Yippee!" Liz squealed and clapped her hands.

Danny broke out into an impromptu song, "Waffles are awesome. Waffles are great. Pile them high up on my plate. Cover them in syrup, so sticky sweet. Waffles are what I love to eat!"

Liz laughed at Danny's song, which she and Danny sang over and over again at each commercial break. When breakfast-for-dinner was nearly ready, Dad asked the kids to set the table. Liz sang the waffle song again as she set the forks and napkins on the table. She reached around Danny who set three plates on the table. She and her brother grabbed the cups of milk Dad had poured for them and brought them carefully to the table.

Sitting down for dinner, Danny said, "It's weird eating dinner without Mom."

"I miss Mommy," Liz said.

"It is weird without Mom, and I miss her, too," Dad said.

"Has she called or texted or anything?" Danny asked.

"Did she forget about us?" Liz asked.

"No and no. She's just busy," Dad said.

"I hope we don't have to wait for Mom to go out of town to have waffles for dinner. I want waffles every night!" Danny said.

"Can we?" Liz asked. "At least until Mommy gets home?"

Dad set the bowl of scrambled eggs and the plate with the mound of waffles on the table. He said, "I don't think you'd like waffles every night."

"Yeah we would!" they said.

"Too much of a good thing isn't always good."

"Uh oh," Danny said, "Here comes another story."

"Daddy, stories are for bedtime," Liz insisted.

THREE BIG WISHES

Once upon a time, a man named Martin strolled through the woods. Martin stopped when he heard a lot of rustling from not too far away. He wasn't sure what made the sound, and hoped it wasn't a bear or a wolf. As he carefully peeked from behind the trees, he caught a strange sight. A squirrel had caught its tail in the forked branches of a sapling and hung upside down. It twisted and squirmed to get itself free, but even after all the effort, the squirrel remained trapped and helpless. Martin cautiously freed the squirrel's tail from the sapling and set the squirrel gently onto the ground. Instead of scampering away, the squirrel stood on its hind legs and bowed to the man.

"Thank you, kind sir," the squirrel said.

"You can talk?" Martin asked, surprised. He had seen many animals on his walks through the woods, but had never encountered a talking one.

"Of course I can. I'm a squirrel, aren't I?" the squirrel said.

"How did your tail get stuck like that?" Martin asked.

"Never mind that. Let's agree never to speak of that embarrassing situation again," the squirrel said. "For saving me, I will grant you three wishes."

"Can I wish for more wishes?" Martin asked.

"No! Of course not! If you want to maximize your wishes, I suggest you make bigger wishes," the squirrel said.

Martin had never heard of a wish-granting squirrel, but he had never known one to talk, either. To humor the squirrel, he thought up three grand wishes.

"For my first one, I wish for a mansion with five hundred rooms."

"No problem," the squirrel said. It swished its tail, crinkled up its nose, and granted Martin's first wish.

"For my second one, I wish one of the rooms in the mansion

contains all sorts of riches."

"Easily done," the squirrel said. It swished its tail, crinkled up its nose, and granted Martin's second wish.

"For my last one, I wish when I ask for food, it will appear before me, so I will never go hungry."

"If that is what you wish," the squirrel said. It swished its tail, crinkled up its nose, and granted Martin's last wish.

"When you return home, you will find your wishes," the squirrel said. It bowed again and then scampered away.

Martin finished his walk and trudged back to his house on the edge of the forest. When he stepped out of the woods, instead of finding his small house, he saw a huge mansion in its place. He could tell it was his house, because his neighbors still had their much smaller houses on either side of his new, larger house, only scooted further down the street to make enough space for his five-hundred-room mansion.

Unfortunately, even though the squirrel did grant his wishes, the wishes were not what Martin expected. His mansion had five hundred rooms, just like he wished. Instead of taking his walk in the woods, Martin spent a day counting each room. With that many rooms, Martin realized he couldn't keep all the rooms clean. He decided to only clean a few of the rooms, the ones he used the most, on a regular basis.

Not many people know this, but when rooms get too dusty, they tend to attract ghosts. After a while of allowing too many rooms get too dusty, a majority of his mansion became haunted by hundreds of ghosts which kept Martin awake at night with their moaning about all the dust build up.

You might think Martin could have used his Room of Riches to hire people to keep his mansion clean. The room did contain all sorts of riches. There were stacks of paper money and coins from all the countries of the world. There were bowls filled with gems and jewels. The walls were decorated with rare artwork from famous painters. There was a metal drum of oil, which made tycoons both filthy and rich. Plus, there was one wooden barrel filled with nuts and acorns, which the squirrel considered the best kind of riches. And seated on a sofa were three men named Rich: Richard Smith, Richard Jones, and Richard Hughes. Unfortunately, the riches, including the Richards, were stuck in the room. An invisible force at the doorway and windows prevented any of the riches (or Richards) from ever leaving.

You might also think Martin could have used his last wish to either feed the Richards or start a restaurant to make money, but he couldn't. It was true that whenever Martin mentioned food, it would appear before him. Unfortunately, he could not share his food with anyone, not even the Richards. When he tried, the food would fly out of the other person's hands and straight into Martin's mouth. A similar thing would happen if Martin didn't finish his food within an hour. He quickly realized how often idioms involved food. Phrases like, "that's nuts" or "It's hotter than a baked potato" would cause nuts or a baked potato to appear before him, even when he wasn't hungry.

Martin lived out the rest of his life in his mostly haunted mansion. Because food might appear, he took a vow of silence, except at meal times. He tried to befriend the Richards, but they despised Martin for imprisoning them in the Room of Riches, where they survived on nothing but nuts from the wooden barrel and the meals Martin prepared the usual way in his kitchen and brought to them three times a day.

Martin continued taking walks in the woods, hoping he could find the talking squirrel, which he never did. In his silence, he thought about his wishes. He learned to be more careful of what to wish for. He decided that bigger is not necessarily better. If he ever encountered the talking squirrel, he would wish for simpler things, like wishing for a friend to share walks in the woods.

"You see? Too much of a good thing isn't always good," Dad said.

"So, you're saying we can't have waffles every night?" Liz asked.

"He's saying we would get tired of waffles if we ate them every night," Danny said.

"Exactly," Dad said.

"Can we have waffles again for breakfast after Mommy gets home?" Liz asked.

"We'll see," Dad said.

"That means 'no'," Danny said to Liz, looking smug.

"That does not mean 'no'. It means I don't know what Mom has planned this weekend, so I don't know if there will be time to make waffles. If we do have time, I'm all for making waffles again."

The kids cheered and sang the waffle song, again.

The Toymaker's Apprentice

A story about taking responsibility.

After dinner, Liz and Danny cleared the plates and Dad rinsed them off in the sink. Dad had to wipe down the table, too, especially Liz's place at the table and her chair which were sticky with syrup.

Liz and Danny went upstairs to play before bedtime. Using a coloring book as a flat surface, Danny stacked blocks to build a castle for his plastic army men to defend.

Liz didn't know what toy she wanted to play with. She only knew she didn't want to build a castle with Danny, because he never thought she built it right. She searched the toy box. She shuffled toys out of the way, but they fell in on themselves. Liz decided to pull the toys out of the box to get them out of the way. With toys piling up around her, she tossed a foam stress ball, the size and shape of an apple, over her shoulder.

"Liz! You knocked it down!" Danny growled.

Liz spun around and yelped, "I didn't do it!"

"Yes, you did!" Danny yell.

"I was over here! How could I break your castle? Maybe you did it!"

"I didn't do it! Why would I break my own castle? You threw that apple at it!"

"I was just getting it out of my way! I wasn't aiming it at your castle!"

They heard Dad's chair scoot back from his desk, followed by footsteps on the stairs.

"Now, you've really done it Liz," Danny said. "Here comes Dad."

Dad appeared at the top of the stairs and asked, "What's going on?"

They both erupted into their sides of the story, blaming each other. Dad stopped them from yelling, but when he asked again what happened, the yelling started all over again.

"Fine!" Dad said, raising his voice. "You leave me no choice, but to tell you the story of the toymaker and his apprentice, and why it is important to take responsibility for your actions."

They both groaned.

THE TOYMAKER'S APPRENTICE

There once was a moderately successful toymaker. He made handcrafted toys, but his sales went up and down like his yo-yos. In the spring and fall, he sold many kites with the coming and going of the winds. The holidays were his busiest season. At any other time, he sold a toy here or there, mostly when a child of the village celebrated a birthday or when visitors came to town.

One night, the toymaker awoke from a wonderful dream. It inspired him to create a brilliant new toy. When he was done creating his new toy, word of its brilliance spread and the toy and its maker became very popular. People, both children and adults, wanted their own to play with, but the toymaker couldn't keep the new toy in ample supply. Customers grew impatient with the toymaker, and demanded he make more of the fabulous toy.

Stressed by the popularity of the new toy, the toymaker had trouble sleeping. When he did finally fall asleep, he had another wonderful dream about a golem. The golem was a large man made out of clay who followed his every command. When he awoke the next day, he closed the toyshop early to work on making the golem from his dream. The toymaker followed his dream as close as he could remember and created the golem to help him keep up with the demands.

The toymaker instructed the golem to build his brilliant new toy. The golem did good work duplicating the toy. Even with its bulky fingers made of clay, the golem was able to construct the tiny pieces of the toy. The new toys continued to sell like crazy.

Eventually, the toyshop ran out of some of the pieces. Supplies were low, and even if the toymaker ordered more supplies, it would take time for the delivery to arrive. The golem, only doing what the toymaker instructed it to do, did not know to stop when there were not enough pieces. It continued making the toys as best as it could without all the necessary pieces.

The toymaker did not know about the incomplete toys and continued to sell as many as he could. Eventually, some people returned to the store to complain about their broken toys. When the toymaker opened the toy to repair it, he immediately could tell that not all the pieces were there. The toymaker was annoyed he had to refund the toys due to missing parts.

When the shop closed, the toymaker, still angry from having to offer so many refunds, yelled at the golem for making broken toys. The golem wanted to explain that it did what it was instructed to do, that it did not have enough parts and tried its best to make new toys with the parts it had, but the toymaker had not given the golem a mouth. The golem tried its best to gesture to the toymaker, but the toymaker did not understand. Frustrated, the toymaker went to bed and left saying, "Tomorrow, I will figure out what to do with the broken toys you made."

As the toymaker slept, the golem tried to fix the broken toys. The workshop was out of spare pieces needed to fix the toys, but other toys in the shop did have the necessary parts. The golem did not want the toymaker to be mad at it anymore, so it took apart some of the other toys to get enough pieces to fix the new toys. By morning, all the new toys had the pieces they needed, and worked perfectly.

When the toymaker arrived at the shop, the golem wanted to show him the fixed toys. Instead, the toymaker was furious the golem had broken the other toys in the shop. He did not understand the golem had used the other toys to fix the new toys, which were in greater demand. Instead, the toymaker assumed the golem must have been mad at being yelled at and took out its anger on the toys. Without a mouth, the golem could not explain what it had done to help the toymaker.

The toymaker looked around his store and only saw broken toys everywhere. He would not be able to open the shop. The golem had harmed his reputation as a toymaker by making incomplete toys and now it had taken apart many of the remaining toys. He did not create an assistant to help him with his toys. He created a monster that destroyed his livelihood. The toymaker decided there was only one thing to do. He must get his hammer and destroy the golem before it could do any more harm.

When the toymaker returned with his hammer, it saw the golem dismantling more toys. The toymaker smacked the golem with the hammer over and over, but the hammer bounced off the hard, clay body of the golem. The golem continued its work while the toymaker hit it over and over, until finally, the golem completed its task.

"Wait!", the golem said with the mouth it had built from bits of toys.

With its new mouth, the golem explained it had tried to make the toys as best it could, but it ran out of parts. It was instructed to make the new toys, but was not instructed to stop if it ran out of pieces. It explained that it found the missing pieces in the other toys and tried to fix what it was told to do. It only wanted to do its best to make the toymaker happy.

The toymaker dropped the hammer. He did know they had run out of pieces and they awaited the order of more spare parts. He should have given the golem better instructions to stop when the pieces ran out. Before he could apologize, cracks spread quickly over the golem's body. The toymaker's assistant crumbled apart all over the floor.

The toymaker dropped to his knees. He felt bad for blaming the golem and for destroying it. He accepted full responsibility for not ordering enough pieces for all the toys and for not giving the golem better instructions. The toymaker cried and cried as he held the broken remains of the golem in his hands. He pleaded for forgiveness and wished he could take back everything he did and said. His tears splashed to the floor, mixing with the clumps of broken clay. Distraught at what he had done, the toymaker stood up slowly and shuffled out of the shop. He would clean up his shop and start to rebuild his livelihood another day.

While the toymaker was away, the broken bits of golem mixed with the toymaker's tears and wishes. The golem reconstructed itself. Eventually, when the golem was fully restored, it worked at rebuilding the toymaker's toys. When the toymaker returned, several of the new toys were in working order. And, even though the shop did not include all the original toys, the golem did its best with what it had to restore as many as it could with the pieces available in the workshop.

The toymaker was happy to see the golem fully restored and apologized for his actions.

With its new mouth, the golem said, "We sometimes make mistakes."

The toymaker agreed and added, "When we do, we take responsibility for those mistakes and do our best to fix them."

"I am sure whatever happened was a mistake. I wasn't up here to see what really happened. Danny, can you tell me what happened?"

"Why are you blaming me? I just went to get more blocks. When I turned around, my castle got knocked over. Liz threw that apple at it."

"I did not!"

"Danny, I am not blaming you. I'm just asking what happened. Did you see the apple hit your castle?" Dad asked.

"No, but it was lying next to it."

"Danny, is it possible something else, like your foot, bumped the comic book and knocked down the castle?"

"It was Lizzie throwing toys out of the box," he said.

Dad took a deep breath, let it out, and said, "That's not what I asked. Is it possible you bumped the comic book?"

"It's a coloring book, Dad. Not a comic book."

Dad gave Danny a stern look, suggesting it was not the most opportune time to be correcting him. "Answer the question."

"Yeah. maybe."

"And, Liz. I know how you can fling toys out of the toy box when you're looking for something."

"But, I didn't—"

Dad raised his hands to stop her. "Is it possible the apple could have hit Danny's castle?"

"Maybe. I guess."

"If both things are possible, then one of you may have accidentally knocked it over. Whatever happened and no matter who did it, take responsibility for your actions, accept the blame, and work on fixing the problem."

"I'm sorry if the apple knocked over your castle," Liz said.

"I might have bumped the coloring book when I went to get

more blocks," Danny said.

"Do you need help rebuilding it?" Liz asked. She doubted he would accept her way of building it, but at least she could hand him the blocks.

"Thanks, Lizzie. I'd like that."

Together, they built a better castle, which they both had fun trying to knock down with the foam apple and two scruffy tennis balls they also found from the bottom of the toy box.

Singing for Supper

A story about following rules.

In her bedroom, as Liz put on her nightshirt, she sang the waffle song. She heard Danny open the bathroom door and groan, "Ugh! Why did I make up that song? Lizzie, you're gonna get it stuck in my head."

"I like your waffle song," she said as she opened the door to her bedroom.

"Did you both brush your teeth?" Dad asked.

"Yep," Danny said. "Just did."

"Why do we always have to brush our teeth?" Liz asked.

"Because, it's good for you, and it's one of the rules," Dad said.

"You and Mom have too many rules," Danny grumbled.

"Some of the rules I learned from your Granny and Grandpa. Just be glad Granny didn't hear you sing at the dinner table. Otherwise, someone might have showed up to take you away," Dad said.

"What?" they asked.

"Don't tell your Granny I let you sing at the dinner table. She used to tell me and my brother people would take us away if they heard us sing at the dinner table."

"What people?" Liz asked. Images of masked robbers cramming kids into large sacks popped into her mind.

"Sometimes it was pirates. Sometimes it was the circus. You know...people."

"That would never happen," Danny said.

"Would it happen?" Liz asked, concerned there might be pirates or clowns lurking somewhere.

Dad shrugged and said, "Probably not. But, it was one of your Granny's rules. Mr. Witherspoon didn't follow the rules, and look what happened to him.."

"Oh no," Danny said.

"Another story?" Liz asked.

"Yes, but this one is from your Granny. I've spiced it up a bit, but the gist of it is still the same."

Danny sighed, "What happened to Mr. Witherspoon?"

"You see, it was like this…"

SINGING FOR SUPPER

There once was a poor, starving man named Mr. Witherspoon, who scrounged for anything to eat wherever he could find food. Sometimes his meals were bits of food that other people threw away, and other times his meals were from one of the homeless shelters. His favorite meals were the ones he could buy for himself.

He didn't have much other than the clothes on his back and a few extra things he kept in a weathered backpack. One of his most treasured possessions was a plastic recorder which was dented and cracked. He played it as often as he could. Mr. Witherspoon would stand on the street corners and sing or play his recorder to the busy traffic passing by. Sometimes, the people in the cars would offer him money. The money made him happy, because he could buy himself something, but nothing made him happier than his music on a sunny day.

One sunny day, Mr. Witherspoon received a special dinner invitation. A few times a year, one of the richest families in town would hold a picnic on their lawn and share their good fortune with the less fortunate. They invited as many poor people as they could to dine with them. Some people refused, because they thought this family was showing off their wealth instead of doing something charitable, but most thought it was very kind of the family and joined them in this celebration of life. The family asked their guests to respect one simple, but important, rule—No one was to sing at the dinner table.

In the gazebo on the family's estate, a band began to entertain the picnic guests. The band played handcrafted instruments as if the members had plucked them out of history. There was a guitar that didn't quite look like a guitar. Instead of the guitar having a figure-eight shaped body, it was more egg shaped with the point at the base of the guitar instead of up at the neck. One musician played a twirly horn with clam-like valves that popped back open when he lifted his fingers. Another musician played a wooden recorder. Mr. Witherspoon admired its craftsmanship. A few women accompanied the band and danced a light-footed jig in a swirl of scarves. They played a very upbeat song which made people want to tap their toes or, if you were more adventurous, dance along.

When it came time to eat, the meal was served family-style. Platters of barbecue and various vegetable side dishes filled the center of the table. When one platter or serving dish was emptied, waiters brought another to the table to replace it. Everyone, family and guests, could eat as much or as little as they wanted—as long as they did not sing at the dinner table.

Mr. Witherspoon sat across from the family's youngest daughter. He helped serve food on her plate before he served himself. The smell of the meal was mouthwatering.

"Thank you and your family for this wonderful meal and celebration," Mr. Witherspoon said.

"Thank you for serving my plate," the young girl said, "And, remember…don't sing."

Mr. Witherspoon smiled at her. He placed his napkin across his lap, just like his mother had taught him decades before. He picked up his knife and fork, and looked over his plate, deciding what to eat first: the roast chicken or the potato salad?

He had not yet taken his first bite, when the band began playing Mr. Witherspoon's favorite song. He loved to sing the same song on the street corners. The song and the sunshine made Mr. Witherspoon so happy, he couldn't help drumming along on the table with his fork and knife. Before he could stop himself, Mr. Witherspoon sang along with the band playing his favorite song. He only sang one line before he saw the youngest daughter's face become pale with horror. He immediately stopped singing. With her jaw dropped open, the girl shook her head sadly at Mr. Witherspoon.

"I'm sorry. It's my favorite song," he explained.

The young girl lowered her head, nibbled at her meal, and avoided making eye contact with Mr. Witherspoon.

In a swirl of scarves, the dancers appeared behind Mr. Witherspoon. He tried to ignore them, but each time he tried to eat, the women swished their scarves between his face and his food, preventing him from eating. One of the women scooped up his plate and danced away with it, while another woman entangled Mr. Witherspoon in scarves.

"I'm sorry, I didn't mean to—," he started to apologize, before a scarf whipped into his mouth and prevented him from saying anything more. The woman's scarves seemed to take on the life of a snake and twisted themselves around his wrists and legs. The dancing women passed the other ends of their scarves to a man standing high above him on stilts. Like a marionette, he led Mr. Witherspoon away from the table and all its food. The scarf in his mouth prevented him from calling for help, but it would have done no good. Everyone thought Mr. Witherspoon was part of the afternoon's show. They all laughed and cheered at his expense.

The man on the stilts led Mr. Witherspoon far away from the picnic. The few possessions he carried were taken away, except for the clothes he wore. It broke his heart to see his recorder taken from him. He was hauled to a large cage in the back of a cart. Two grey horses pulled the cart and led a caravan of wagons and carts away from the picnic. Mr. Witherspoon could see other carts with other cages with other people who sang at other dinner tables. Plenty of the caged people cried and wailed, but no one sang now. The caravan traveled across a field and high into the mountains. Mr. Witherspoon had no idea he lived anywhere near mountains. He had never seen mountains in the distance from the city. He never traveled much, and preferred to stay on his favorite street corner to perform to the passing cars. He didn't feel like performing anymore.

The air had turned cool and crisp when the caravan stopped high up in the mountains. He and the other dinner table singers were released from the cages and told to stand in a line. A large man with a bushy, black beard walked slowly up the line, inspecting all the people. He had baggy pants and a puffy white shirt. He wore two brightly colored scarves: one tied around his waist like a belt, and the other around his neck like a tie. Mr. Witherspoon thought he looked like a pirate. This man was the King of the Sky People.

"I look at you and can tell each of you have been very naughty," he bellowed, wagging his fat finger at them in shame. He spoke broken English in a foreign accent. Not getting out much, Mr. Witherspoon imagined it sounded Russian. "You sing at dinner table. Now I own you. You will gather clouds for me? I will teach new song to you. You sing new song. You sing good? I give food to you. You sing bad? No food. Now, go. Gather clouds."

The line of dinner table singers were led away from the caravan to a field at the top of the mountain. Short blades of grass grew in the field at the top of the mountain. Pure white and fluffy clouds broke free from the clouds high above, trotted down to the field, and grazed on the grass like puffy sheep. From high up in the mountain, Mr. Witherspoon could tell all the clouds in the sky were made up of herds of these puffy, cloud sheep.

A couple of the teenaged Sky People taught the imprisoned rule-breakers how to sneak up behind a cloud and gently pick it up as it grazed. Most of the clouds could be caught peacefully, but the ones that didn't want to be caught as easily turned grey and shocked the person holding it with tiny arcs of lightning.

After gathering enough clouds and loading them into the carts that had brought the prisoners to the mountaintop, it was finally time to eat. The king returned and taught them the new song they were to sing in order to get their meal. Mr. Witherspoon was starving by the time it was his turn to sing. He felt tired and did not feel like singing, but he sang the song as best he could.

"Very good," the king said. He nodded to one of his subjects who handed Mr. Witherspoon a plate of food.

The meal did not look nearly as appetizing as the picnic food. There was a slice of moon cheese and a mound of cloud scooped onto his plate. He thought the moon cheese tasted very bland, and the cloud tasted watery. Some people's cloud had a touch of lightning in it. They said it gave the bland food a bit of extra flavor, but it burned their tongue.

For years, Mr. Witherspoon slaved away on the mountaintop, gathering clouds. He never knew what they used the clouds for, and no one felt brave enough to ask. On one occasion, Mr. Witherspoon grew tired of singing the king's song for his meal. Instead, he sang his favorite song. The song he sang on his street corner long ago and far away—The song he started to sing at the dinner table before the Sky

People took him away.

"No good. Wrong song," the king said. He took the plate from the server and flung it off the mountain. The plate streaked across the sky like a shooting star.

At nights, the prisoners slept under the stars and reminisced about their lives before singing at the dinner table. Not all of them were poor and homeless, like Mr. Witherspoon. A few of the people were ones who worked for the wealthy family who held the picnic. Others were the family's friends. And others were strangers who didn't know anything about the picnic, but were taken from their own homes for singing at their own dinner tables. Exhausted from gathering clouds all day, they all slept peacefully under the blanket of stars.

One day, a young woman had hiked to the top of the mountain. She paused a moment to rest and take in the view. She watched the group of people collect clouds and store them into cages. And then, the young woman walked over to Mr. Witherspoon who dripped with sweat and cloud. The young woman smiled at Mr. Witherspoon. He felt uncomfortable having such attention and did his best to ignore her. The young woman removed her backpack, opened it up, and pulled out a plastic recorder. She gave the recorder to Mr. Witherspoon and said, "I warned you not to sing at the dinner table."

Even though many years had passed, he recognized his recorder. It had faded with age, but was the same dented and cracked recorder he played on his favorite street corner so long ago. It took him a moment, but Mr. Witherspoon finally recognized the young woman as the family's youngest daughter who sat across from him at the picnic many years ago. She was older now, and how much she had grown made him realize how long he had been imprisoned on this mountaintop.

"Play me a song, and make it a good one," she said.

"I know just the one," Mr. Witherspoon said, and he began to play his favorite tune on his recorder. The clouds cleared and the sun came out to shine on the mountaintop.

The Sky People could not help themselves. They began to dance to the song. As long as Mr. Witherspoon continued to play, the Sky People continued to dance. They were too busy dancing to punish him and could not force him to continue gathering clouds.

"Let's get you out of here," the young woman said. "Keep playing."

Even though the mountain air was thin and his head felt dizzy, Mr. Witherspoon continued playing. He followed the young woman all the way down the mountain. The young woman drove Mr. Witherspoon into town and dropped him off at his favorite street corner. He was happy to be home again, but almost didn't recognize his corner. A new restaurant had replaced one of his favorite places to eat. A lot more traffic passed by. A new sidewalk and bike path crossed his corner, too.

Before driving away, the young woman invited Mr. Witherspoon to her family's picnic. Mr. Witherspoon said he would love to go, and the young woman agreed to pick him up and drive him to the picnic on the day of the event. Older and wiser, Mr. Witherspoon could not wait to go.

At the picnic, the band played their lively music from the gazebo. They waved, winked, and smiled at Mr. Witherspoon. Not pleased to see the Sky People's band, Mr. Witherspoon at least acknowledged their presence with a polite nod. A young boy smudged with dirt and wearing shabby, torn clothes sat next to Mr. Witherspoon at the table. He could see the boy tapping his feet against his chair to the beat of the music.

Mr. Witherspoon leaned over and told the boy, "I can tell you like this song, but never, ever sing at the dinner table. Take it from somebody who knows. There is a time to eat and a time to sing. Now is the time to eat."

"But, I love this song," the boy protested. He was about to sing along, but Mr. Witherspoon crammed a bread roll into the boy's mouth to stop him.

"Save the song for after dessert, away from the dinner table."

"Did Granny really tell you that story? Or, is it something you made up?" Liz asked.

"She did. But, I think she really told us that story to make my brother and I behave ourselves at the table. Sometimes people make up rules that we don't always understand, but are there for reasons. Like brushing your teeth. You may not understand how brushing your teeth helps keep you healthy, but making it a rule helps build good habits."

"Do you think moon cheese would make a good grilled cheese sandwich?" Danny asked.

"I don't know. What do you think?" Dad asked.

"Probably not. Too moldy," Danny said, sticking out his tongue.

"I'd like to try a scoop of cloud. I bet it tastes like angel food cake or ice cream," Liz said, licking her lips.

"Tomorrow, sing at the dinner table, and maybe you'll get to try some," Danny said.

Liz stuck her tongue out at Danny. She dodged the stuffed animal Danny tossed at her.

"If anyone does sing at the dinner table, I won't let anyone take either of you away," Dad said.

"What about pirates?" Liz asked.

"Oh, they can take all the pirates they want."

"No. I mean, what if pirates take us away?"

"Do the pirates have swords?"

"Well, yeah. Of course. They are pirates," Danny said.

"In that case, I hope you don't get seasick."

"Dad!"

"Good night, kids."

The Missing Page

A story about paying attention

and following instructions.

Dad fixed the kids a plate of apple slices and string cheese as an afternoon snack, and set it on the table between them. Danny grabbed a couple slices of apple and one of the cheese sticks. Liz only ate a cheese stick, even though she complained she was starving on the ride home. Danny gave her a chance to have some of the apples, too, but her homework captured her attention more than the snacks. One by one, Danny ate the other apple slices. No amount of apple slices or cheese sticks could comfort him from his frustrating homework.

Danny growled as he furiously erased parts of his homework. It didn't help he was anxious to do other things. He wanted to get the homework right the first time, but the instructions confused him.

"Argh!" he roared, and shoved his homework away from him.

"What's wrong, Danny?" Dad asked.

"It's this stupid homework! I don't get it!"

"What do the instructions say to do?"

"It just says to fill in the blanks!"

"Okay. Alright. What are you supposed to use to fill in the blanks?"

"Words, but I don't know which ones. Here. Look. It's stupid!" he said, and shoved his homework towards his Dad.

Dad picked up Danny's homework. Danny pointed out his confusion. There was a list of sentences, but not all of them seemed to be related to the same subject. Each sentence had at least one blank, some had two, and seemed vague about what words to use. Dad flipped the page over and Danny pointed out there was no vocabulary list or story associated with the sentences.

Liz looked up with mild interest, but went back to her own homework.

"Do you fill in the blanks with your own words?"

Danny shrugged.

"What about your spelling words?"

"No. None of the spelling words match."

"Then, what are you supposed to use to fill in the blanks?"
Dad asked.

"I don't know! That's why it's stupid!"

"Okay. What did your teacher tell you to do?"

Danny mumbled something.

"Could you repeat that a little louder?" Dad asked.

"I said, I don't remember."

"I understand you're frustrated. Not paying attention when instructions are given can cause big problems. You might end up like the missing page."

"I don't know if my homework is missing a page," Danny said.

"Not that kind of page. I am talking about a king's page, someone who runs errands and delivers messages for the king. It was important for the king's page to listen carefully, but he didn't and he found himself in trouble."

Danny pushed aside his homework and listened to his dad's story. Listening to one of Dad's crazy stories was far better than working on this frustrating assignment. Liz set down her pencil to listen to the story, too.

THE MISSING PAGE

Once upon a time, a long time ago, there were two kings: the king of the humans and the king of the faeries. The kings feuded for many years, because the king of the humans didn't tolerate magic ever since his queen received a pair of magic shoes allowing her to dance among the clouds in the sky. The queen spent most of her time in the sky with the birds, and not enough time on the ground with the people of the kingdom. Since that day, the king of the humans refused to let the faeries and their kind mingle with the human world. As the years passed, the king of the humans had a change of heart when he realized his intolerance of magic was because he was jealous, and he should never be jealous of anything bringing such happiness to his wife.

The feud between humans and faeries approached a boiling point. If the king of humans did not do something soon, war would break out in the borderlands. The human king decided to send an urgent message of peace to the faerie king to prevent the war. He sent for his page, and issued him explicit instructions on how to reach the faerie king.

"On your journey, you will encounter the same crossroads three times, which is why you must follow my instructions. Do you understand?"

"Of course, sire. Right away," the page said.

Unfortunately, the page did not pay attention to the king's instructions. The court jester, a young woman from the nearby village, had distracted the page by making faces and flirting with him. The page was confident and cocky. He thought he would impress the court jester by declaring he could remember the king's instructions. He was so sure he had understood the instructions, he refused the king's offer to have the instructions written down. He took the king's message, tucked it into his shirt pocket, and left immediately.

When the page arrived at the first crossroads, he got very confused and disoriented. The faerie king built the crossroads using magic to confuse and turn around any traveler wanting to reach his kingdom. However, the faerie king always welcomed communication with the human king, despite their differences. Long ago, before the queen received her magic shoes, the faerie king had sent one of his subjects to the human king to provide explicit instructions for how to travel the crossroads connecting the two kingdoms. By not following the instructions, travelers could easily get turned around and lost.

The page looked at each of the four roads extending from the crossroad. Each path looked exactly alike, including the path he had taken to get there. Each path looked like the same country lane with the same barn and same old oak tree off in the distance. Because the page still thought about the beautiful court jester, he didn't remember passing an oak tree or a barn along the way. And, what did the king tell him? Which path was he supposed to take? Left, right, or straight? He was so confused. What would his king say if he went back to ask the king to repeat his instructions, when he refused the first time and felt so confident? Besides, the message was urgent. He would waste too much time traveling back to his king's castle. The longer he worried about not having the correct instruction, the more time would be lost. He feared his mistake would bring the two kingdoms closer to an unnecessary war.

He wished he could remember the directions. What it two rights and a left? Or, was it two lefts and a right? He was positive the faerie king's castle was either a right turn or a left. That much he was sure of. He took the path on the left and walked down a short ways. The barn and the old oak tree faded from view and the road eventually wound its way through a swamp. The page did not remember the king saying anything about a swamp. He figured that way couldn't be correct. He turned around and returned to the crossroads. He walked straight through the crossroads, because that would take him to the path on the right. Again, the barn and old oak tree faded from view and the road eventually wound its way into a desert with sand blowing across the road. The desert didn't seem right, either. Again, the page turned around and returned to the crossroads. Because each direction looked exactly like the other, when he returned, the page was so turned around and confused. He couldn't remember which was the original path he had taken. Filled with worry, the page sat down in the middle of the crossroads, covered his face with his hands, and began to cry.

"What's wrong, lad?" a kind voice asked him.

The page looked up and saw an old man wearing a weathered

cloak over his head. He stood in front of the page, leaning heavily against his walking stick. Although the cloak covered most of his face, he could see the old man smiled kindly through a thick beard.

The page got to his feet and said, "I have an urgent message from my king to be delivered to the king of faeries. Unfortunately, I am all turned around and can't remember how to get to the faerie king's castle."

"Do you have a map?" the old man asked.

The page lowered his head and said, "No. I was too foolish and sure of myself, that I refused."

"Do you have the address?" the old man asked.

"No. My king told me where to go, but he did not have my full attention," the page said, his face turning red thinking about the court jester.

"Are you sure?" the old man asked. He tapped the page's shirt pocket with the letter.

The page was not sure. He had taken the king's message and tucked it into his pocket without much of a glance. He pulled out the message to be delivered to the faerie king and another piece of paper tumbled out. When the page picked up the other paper and unfolded it, the piece of paper had the directions to the other castle. His king was wise enough to provide directions to the other castle anyway. The page felt so happy he started to dance. His dancing stopped when he realized he was still very much turned around and wasn't sure which path to take.

The old man offered to help the page and accompanied him on his journey. The directions were neither two rights and a left, nor two lefts and a right. It said the faerie king designed the crossroads to confuse travelers. The instructions instructed him to travel straight until he reached the same crossroads. From there, take the right path until reaching the same crossroads again, and finally take the left path to reach the other castle.

The old man pointed them down the correct path. Instead of turning into a swamp or a desert, the two walked past the barn and the old oak tree and arrived at the crossroads where each path looked exactly the same. They turned right, walked down the road, again passing the same barn and old oak tree. When they reached the crossroads the third time, they took the road on the left. As they approached the barn and old oak tree, the tree and barn turned into the archway for the faerie king's castle entrance.

They stopped before the archway and the old man said, "This is where I leave you, lad."

"Thank you very much, sir. How can I ever repay you?" the page asked.

The old man tossed back the hood of the cloak and pulled off the thick beard. It wasn't an old man at all, but the court jester in disguise. She said, "You can repay me by paying attention when instructions are given next time. I am sorry for distracting you. Go now, and deliver the message."

The court jester gave the page a gentle kiss on his cheek and wished him luck. She promised to wait for him by the archway to accompany him on their journey home.

The page arrived at the faerie king's castle in time and delivered the letter. The faerie king appreciated the news. War had been averted and peace spread across both kingdoms.

Before he and the court jester headed home, the page asked for directions back to the his king's castle. He paid close attention, wrote the directions down, sketched a map, and clarified everything before departing. He learned to pay attention when instructions were given and to never be afraid to ask for help.

"Can I see your homework, again?" Dad asked. Danny handed him the homework and Dad read it a second time. The instructions only said, "Fill in the blanks", but did not say what words to use.

"Is this the only page?" Dad asked.

Danny grumbled, but dug through his backpack. He found a second page of homework crammed and crinkled at the bottom of the bag. Dad helped him straighten the paper on the table, smoothing out the wrinkles as much as possible. The other part of the homework contained four boxes of text and a list of vocabulary words at the bottom of the page. The homework was not copied properly and many of the words across the entire page were faded and illegible.

"Are you supposed to read what's in the boxes and use words from the list?" Dad asked.

Danny threw his hands up in defeat.

"Tomorrow morning, ask your teacher for help." Dad said.

"What if I get a bad grade?" he whined.

"I'm not worried. This is just one grade. It's not a test. Just a bit of homework. Besides, if all the copies of the second page are like this, there are probably other kids who are confused, too. Maybe the teacher made a mistake. It happens. It's best to ask for help to clear the confusion."

"But—!"

"Daniel, talk to you teacher. She is there to help."

Danny sighed and said, "Okay."

"And, Dan..."

"Yeah, Dad?"

"Next time, please treat your homework with more care."

"Sorry," he said, shrinking behind his backpack.

Take Away the Target

A story about one possible

way to handle a bully.

In another rare moment, Danny and Liz talked about school without Dad asking probing questions about their day.

Danny asked Liz, "Did you hear about Evan and Marshal?"

"Were they the ones that got in trouble for fighting?" Liz asked.

Danny nodded. "Evan threw Marshal's lunchbox into a tree."

"Why did Evan throw Marshal's lunchbox into a tree?" Dad asked.

Danny shook his head and grumbled, "Because Evan is a jerk."

"Yeah," Liz agreed, "I hate him."

"Whoa. Why the strong words?" Dad asked.

They told Dad how Evan picks on people. Danny said his class and Evan's share the same recess, and Evan is always sitting out because he stirs up so much trouble. Liz said he has made fun of her and her friends in the hallway.

"He sounds like a bully," Dad said, "Do you know how to deal with bullies?"

"Have ninjas take him down?" Danny suggested.

"Throw him into a volcano?" Liz suggested.

"Ninjas or a volcano? Why not tell the teacher?" Dad asked.

"The teacher knows. She doesn't do much about it. He still bullies kids."

"Have you tried ignoring him?" Dad asked.

"Evan is hard to ignore," Liz said.

"Ignoring him makes him try harder," Danny said.

"Have you tried taking away his target?" Dad asked.

"We can't all just run and hide from him," Danny said.

"Other than running and hiding, there are other ways to

take away his target."

"Like martial arts?"

"Not what I was thinking," Dad said, "Bullies pick weak targets to make themselves feel stronger. Bullies usually target people physically weaker. Some people don't want to confront the bully, and think it's easier to give in to their demands. When people are more evenly matched, the bully does something to make their victim seem weaker. Like the lunchbox...Marshal probably has a nice lunchbox and Evan doesn't. So, Evan threw Marshal's into the tree, and now Marshal feels weaker because something of his was taken away"

"'I kind of see what you're saying," Danny said.

"I don't," Liz said.

"Do you have any stories about taking away a bully's target?" Danny asked.

"Let me think," Dad said. "I've got one."

TAKE AWAY THE TARGET

Back in ancient times when gods and monsters walked among humans, a minotaur bullied a kingdom. Minotaurs were half man and half bull, and most were peaceful creatures. In fact, many minotaurs worked as ranchers, because they could speak the languages of humans and cattle. This story is about one, very mean minotaur. He may have been half bull, but he was full bully.

The minotaur strutted into town one day. The king heard frequent complaints about this bully tormenting his subjects. Parents claimed the minotaur shoved and kicked their children. The farmers reported the chickens would no longer lay eggs because the minotaur stepped on them. The farmers also said he wrestled the pigs, then washed off the mud in the town-square fountain. The minotaur picked fights with people of all ages and social classes.

For a while, the king encouraged his subjects to just ignore the minotaur's bullying and figured he would eventually get bored and leave town. But, the minotaur did not stop his bullying. When the minotaur interrupted and heckled the king's speech, the king decided enough was enough. The bullying must stop.

First, the king sent his scholars and philosophers to reason with the minotaur, but they could not reason with a creature who spoke nothing but lies, insults, and argued against every word they said. There was absolutely no talking sense into the beast. The scholars and philosophers returned to the king with the bad news.

Next, the king asked the priests to have their followers pray for the beast to change its evil ways and to live a happier life. The faithful took to the streets to pray for the minotaur's soul, but the minotaur mocked the church folk and made several of the followers question their beliefs. The priests prayed to their gods for help. The gods replied the minotaur tested their faith. To interfere with the test would be cheating and the devout would learn nothing.

Finally, the king figured if the minotaur could not be reasoned with nor rehabilitated, it was time to deploy force. He sent his best knights to tame the wild creature. The minotaur fought dirty and the knights returned defeated with their armor dented.

"I am out of ideas, and none of the ones I had worked," the king said, "What am I to do?"

"This bully is not—*fooling*—around, is he sire?" the jester jested, attempting to lighten the king's mood.

"This is no joking matter, jester! We have a serious problem," the king said, scowling. Then, the king's mood lightened. He stared at the jester and stroked his chin. "Perhaps you could help."

"M-m-me, sire?" the jester squeaked.

The king nodded. "Perhaps this serious problem requires a less serious solution."

"I am merely the court jester. I tell jokes and act silly. How can I possibly help?"

The jester thought the king must surely be joking, but he was not about to tell him that. "I believe in you, jester. I am certain you can help. Make it so!"

The jester swallowed down his fear and bowed deep to his king.

"May the gods watch over you," the king said, as the jester left the throne room.

What did the jester know about handling bullies? He was not strong? He could be witty, but if the king's wisest scholars and philosophers couldn't talk down the bully, what could he say? He only dealt with hecklers. Maybe the bully was no worse than the worst of all hecklers.

Hecklers often made fun of the jester by teasing him as he entertained. The jester knew a thing or two about teasing people. He often teased people for laughs. When the jester teased people, he made them a target. He could read the room to understand who didn't mind being a target and would stop when his jokes had gone too far. When the jester knew he went too far and his jokes crossed the line, he would make himself the target, instead. The minotaur, on the other hand, was a bully. He would go too far for glory and power. The minotaur targeted the weak, or used his power against stronger targets to make them feel weak. The king was right. The jester did know how to handle the minotaur—by controlling the minotaur's targets.

The jester focused on the weakest targets first, like children and small animals. He taught the children how to climb trees when the minotaur approached. Minotaurs could not climb trees because their horns caught on the branches.

Next, he worked with farmers to protect the chickens. Together, they constructed a series of platforms on the side of the farm house and trained the chickens to climb the ramps to feed on the roof. The platforms were too small and the minotaur was too heavy to climb to the roof.

The jester continued through the town, helping people who had been bullied learn how not to be a target. Many people were upset they had to change their lifestyles or routines just to avoid being tormented by the minotaur. People shouldn't have to change how they speak or what they wear or anything about themselves because of bullies. The people of the kingdom celebrated each other's differences, and some even tried to show the minotaur how to appreciate one another. Unfortunately, bullies are often set in their ways, and the minotaur was happiest when he made other people miserable. The people were still not happy about changing because of a bully. The jester assured them the changes were only temporary, and once the minotaur was no longer a threat, they could all go back to their normal differences.

Removing as many targets as he could was the first phase of the jester's plan. With most of the targets diminished, the jester went to the town square where he could make himself a target. The jester wore a ridiculous outfit of many bright and clashing colors. He loudly sang a song he made up. His song was not particularly good, did not rhyme, and often out of tune. As he sang, he danced around the town square in an uncoordinated way and not to the beat of his own music, which did not have much rhythm anyway. By doing all these crazy things, he made himself the most obvious target in the kingdom.

By the time the minotaur arrived, its frustration had increased at not finding a suitable target in which to bully. When he spotted the jester, he felt like someone remembered his birthday.

"What do we have here?" the minotaur asked, chuckling to himself about the jester.

The jester stopped his song for a moment to answer, "Just a fool, singing and dancing."

"Singing? You call that singing? I've heard better sounds from a dying goat," the minotaur said, laughing.

"That's because goats don't know the words," the jester said, smiling at the minotaur.

"Your lyrics don't even rhyme," the minotaur said with a sneer.

The jester cocked his head to the side and said, "If you think my rhyming is bad, you should taste my cooking."

The minotaur continued to poke fun at the jester, but the jester deflected each insult with a joke about himself. The minotaur insulted the jester's clothes, and the jester found it humorous. The minotaur targeted the jester's dancing; the jester responded with a joke. As this banter went back and forth between the two, the minotaur grew more annoyed that he could not upset the jester. Where was the fun in bullying someone if the insults rolled right off? Realizing he could not outwit the jester with insults, the minotaur decided to rough him up and steal his hat.

The minotaur swiped at the jester's floppy hat.

"Oh ho! You want my hat?" the jester asked, shaking his head and jingling the bells on the pointy ends. "You'll have to catch me first!"

The minotaur grabbed at the hat again, but the jester ducked and dodged the minotaur's massive, outstretched hands. The jester trotted away, down the street, jingling his hat as he fled.

"Come back here, little man!" the minotaur roared.

"Catch me if you can," the jester sang.

The minotaur chased the jester through the streets of town. He could easily follow, because even when the jester was out of sight, he listened for the jingling bells on the jester's hat. He followed the jester through the gated entrance of the garden at the edge of town. The garden had high stone walls with creeping vines growing over them.

The walls of the garden wandered this way and that, like a labyrinth, which is a fancy word for, "maze." The scholars enjoyed walking through the garden quietly thinking to themselves. Young couples strolled through the garden, hand-in-hand, and fell in love. Children liked playing hide-and-seek in the garden. The jester had another idea for the garden.

"I've got you now, little man," the minotaur bellowed as he entered the garden maze.

The minotaur thought he had cornered the jester in the garden, but what he did not know was the jester had scaled a trellis on the far side of the garden and escaped. As the minotaur wandered deeper into the maze, the king ordered the garden gates to be sealed.

The king patted the jester on the back and said, "I never doubted you. Thank you for taking care of this bully."

"Now we know who the real fool is, don't we sire?" the jester said.

"Indeed we do," the king agreed.

The people were upset to lose their garden to the minotaur, but it was a small price to pay to no longer be bullied. The king gave the minotaur an open offer that he was free to go whenever he wanted, as long as he agreed to stop his bullying. The minotaur, like most bullies, was too set in his ways and turned down the offer by insulting the king.

From that moment on, the minotaur forever wandered the labyrinth hoping for new targets to bully.

"Great story, Daddy, but how does that help us with Evan?" Liz asked.

"When Evan tries to make fun of you and your friends, instead of getting upset about it, find the ridiculousness of what he's picking on and defuse it with humor. That way, you appear stronger than him. When you can make fun of yourself, it takes away his target."

"What if he tries to take our things to throw into a tree?" Danny asked.

"I don't know. Maybe tell him trees don't like playing catch. Or, tell him trees likes playing tag instead, especially when they can be base," Dad said.

Liz and Danny laughed.

Danny said, "Dad, that's after he's thrown something into a tree. Marshal and his friends spent most of recess throwing balls to knock down the lunchbox."

"Sounds like they invented a new game...tree ball," Dad suggested.

Danny rolled his eyes and shook his head.

Dad said, "Most likely, Evan does stuff like that because he doesn't know better ways of getting attention. Show him a better way."

"Is that why you're telling us these stories?" Danny asked.

"What? To get attention? You asked for a story about bullies."

Danny took a deep breath and said, "Yeah, but I feel like I'm the target of your other stories."

"Do you think I'm bullying you by telling these stories?" Dad asked.

"Not exactly bullied, but it seems like most of your stories were meant for me. And, I'm not a bad kid."

"Oh, Danny, no. I don't think either of you are bad kids.

The stories are for both you and Liz. Sometimes, you both need reminders. Your mom has her way of explaining things. My stories are how I explain things by making them more relatable. They're not to pick on anyone. I am sorry if they made you feel that way."

"Thanks, Dad," Danny said. He got up and gave Dad a hug. Liz stood up, also. She needed a hug, too.

Out of Bounds

A story about respecting boundaries.

After dinner, the house was quiet. Dad used this tranquil moment to focus on work. Liz and Danny played in their own rooms. Liz laid on her bed, lost in her imagination playing with her stuffed animals. Danny reread one of his favorite Spider Man comics. Suddenly, Liz shattered the silence.

"Danny! Where's my yoyo?"

Liz barged into Danny's room to look for her yoyo. This was not the traditional walk-the-dog, around-the-world kind of yoyo. This was a button-yoyo Liz and her mom had made. Liz found a button at school. Mom had shown her how to thread a loop of string through the holes of the button. By pulling and loosening the string, the yoyo alternated spinning one way, and then the other.

Danny lowered his comic, "I don't have your stupid yoyo! Get out of my room!"

"You played with it last!"

"Yeah, and I gave it back to you. I don't know what you did with it. Go make a mess of your own room, and leave my stuff alone."

"Maybe I'll just take something of yours until you give me my yoyo back." She eyed his action figures, deciding which one she should claim.

The argument quickly escalated into another shouting match. Neither got loud enough to make Liz's yoyo magically appear, but it didn't stop them from trying.

"You took it out of my room to play with it!" Liz screamed.

"That was yesterday. I gave it back!" Danny yelled. "Put that down! I told you I don't have it!"

Danny followed Liz and his action figure into Liz's room. A moment later, Dad appeared in the hallway outside the bedroom door. The moment they saw Dad, they each approached the doorway with their side of the argument as loud as possible. It *had yet to sink in with either of them, no matter how many times Mom or Dad told them: volume doesn't win the argument.*

Dad asked Liz, "Where did you last see your yoyo?"

"I saw Danny go into my room yesterday to play with it."

"Danny?"

"I played with it, but I put it back where I found it," he said, shrugging. "Now, she thinks she can take my toys!"

The argument erupted once more. Dad held up his hands to stop them. He pointed to Liz's bed and said, "Both of you, sit."

When they were seated on Liz's bed among the herd of animals, Dad said, "There once was an empty lot next to a creepy house..."

"Dad, are you saying a ghost took my yoyo?" Liz asked.

"Shush. Listen..."

OUT OF BOUNDS

There once was an empty lot next to a creepy house. Whoever lived there did not keep up with the house's appearance. The paint was chipped and some of the bricks were cracked. The house rarely had lights on, and the ones turned on glowed dim and yellow. The only things growing more than the yard's weeds were the wild rumors about the house and its occupant.

Most of the neighborhood kids believed the house was haunted. A few believed the house had been abandoned many years ago. The kids who played in the empty lot believed an old witch lived in the house.

One day, the kids gathered to play a game of kickball in the empty lot. Crazy Legs Jimmy kicked the ball too wild and too hard and the ball flew over the fence and into the overgrown backyard of the creepy house.

The kids argued about who was at fault and who should go get the ball. Speedy, the pitcher, should get the ball for rolling it too fast. No, Crazy Legs should get the ball for kicking it too crazy. No, Sleepy Tina, the outfielder, should have tried to stop the ball from flying over the fence. Zombie Food, the brains of the gang, usually had good ideas. He suggested they wait for the next half moon, because that is when witches are at their weakest. Boogers stepped forward with another suggestion. He was nicknamed "Boogers" because in art class he had sticky bits of glue all over his fingers that looked like boogers, and not because he picked his nose. Since Boogers was next to be the kicker, he volunteered to get the ball.

A silence fell over the group as they watched Boogers approach the house next door to get the ball back. They watched him knock on the door. Someone answered, but no one could see who opened the door. Despite what the kids were told by their parents and teachers about entering a stranger's house, Boogers went inside.

None of the kids wore a watch, so no one was sure how long he was in the house. As the time passed, they began to worry something horrible had happened to him.

"Did anyone see who answered the door?" Speedy asked.

"Do you think the witch got him?" Sleepy Tina asked, yawning.

"My dad says houses like that have weak floorboards. He might have broke through the floor and is stuck in the basement," Zombie Food said.

"Maybe one of us should go check on him," Crazy Legs said.

"Why? I'm right here," Boogers said, walking up behind the group with the ball tucked under his arm.

The kids stared at Boogers with mouths open.

"What happened? What happened?" the other kids asked.

"I just—" Boogers started to say, but was interrupted.

"Did you meet the witch?"

"Or, was it the ghost?"

"Is the house just as creepy inside?"

"Did your foot break through a loose floorboard?"

They shared what horrible things they imagined had happened to the him, but each were too busy telling their own version of the story, none of them listened to Boogers as he tried to explain what really had happened when he went to fetch the ball. He soon gave up trying to explain his side of the story and let the other kids believe what they wanted to believe.

King Wally, the self-proclaimed leader of the group and official nickname issuer, stepped forward and said, "That was a brave thing you did. As the King, your new name is Fearless."

The other kids patted Fearless on the back before playing more kickball.

Several days later, the same thing happened again. Speedy rolled the ball too fast and Crazy Legs kicked the ball over the fence. This time, King Wally, who was jealous of Fearless's act of bravery, declared he would get the ball himself.

King Wally walked up to the house and knocked on the door. He waited, and then knocked on the door again. No one answered, not even a ghost or a witch.

King Wally walked around to the fence enclosing the backyard. He climbed up the fence and sat on the edge looking down into the backyard. "Whoa," he said quietly to himself. The grass in the backyard stood at least a foot high with weeds and wilted plants standing even taller. He spotted the ball flattening the grass about midway across the yard. Hoping not to land on anything hidden in the tall grass, King Wally leapt down into the yard and shuffled his way through the grass.

He bent down to pick up the ball, but when he stood up again, he heard rustling noises in the grass. After watching too many nature videos in science class, King Wally thought about tigers! That was ridiculous. The backyard couldn't have tigers. Then, his mind suggested, "What about snakes?"

Standing in the middle of the yard, the fence seemed miles away, but the creepy, old house seemed closer. King Wally fled to the small patio outside the house's back door. He looked at the fence and then at the rustling in the grass. There was more than one thing moving around unseen in the grass. That's when King Wally thought about another dangerous animal—Sharks!

As panic filled King Wally, he spun around and knocked on the door. Without waiting more than a second, he tried the handle. The door was unlocked, so he let himself inside and slammed the door shut again. He looked out the window into the yard, and backed away from the door. Something cold brushed against his arm as he backed up. King Wally yelped.

He spun around and saw that he brushed up against a stone statue of a dog resting on short table. The statue wobbled back and forth. Then, as if watching it in slow motion, the stone dog toppled over, fell off the table and crashed to the floor, breaking into hundreds of stone chunks. King Wally yelped, again.

"Hello? Is someone there?" a voice creaked from upstairs.

"The witch!" King Wally thought. He sprinted through the strange house to the front door. He didn't stop running until he was back in the empty lot. The other kids demanded to know about King Wally's adventures. He told them about the snakes that almost got him in the backyard, how the witch had petrified one of the neighbor's dogs, and how she nearly petrified him, too, for sneaking into her house. The other kids believed every word King Wally said. Only Fearless had his doubts.

After hearing about King Wally's adventures, the other kids couldn't wait to have an adventure of their own.

"You can't go over there now. She'll be expecting us," King Wally said.

"Like waiting for hornets to settle down after disturbing their nest?" Zombie Food asked.

"Exactly. We'll go tomorrow," King Wally said.

"I don't think that's a good idea," Fearless said.

"That doesn't sound very fearless of you. Do you want to go back to being called, 'Boogers'?" King Wally asked.

Fearless shook his head. It wasn't that Fearless was afraid of going to the house. He thought they all should leave the woman who lived there alone. Sneaking into her backyard and home was a terrible idea.

The next day, the kids gathered in the empty lot. Everyone except Fearless.

"I guess Fearless chickened out," King Wally said. "We'll sneak in the back."

The kids went to the fence surrounding the backyard. They heard noises coming from the yard. They pressed their faces to the fence and looked through knots in the fence and between the wooden slats. Fearless was already at the witch's house. He was in the backyard raking up the tall grass he had helped mow. Fearless worked as if in a trance. The kids watched an old woman shuffle out the back door, set a cup down on a small table, and shuffle back inside. After Fearless finished raking the last pile of grass, he walked over to the small table and drank from the cup. Still as if in a trance, Fearless walked with the cup into the house.

The kids feared what the witch's potion might do to Fearless. They decided whatever was in the cup put Fearless into his trance. Should they rescue Fearless? Should they confront the witch? They decided to face the witch, even if she turned them into stone. Zombie Food suggested if the witch was going to turn them all into stone, it was better to be where other neighbors could see. King Wally led them to the front of the house. They pounded on the front door.

After several seconds of banging on the door, an elderly woman answered. "Yes? May I help you?" she croaked.

The kids waited for King Wally to say something to the old woman, but he stood there in stunned silence after coming face-to-face with the witch.

Crazy Legs broke the silence when he pointed into the house and said, "Look!"

The others looked where Crazy Legs pointed. Up against the wall in the foyer, they saw a statue of a boy that looked like Fearless. The witch had turned him to stone—even after he finished doing yard work for her!

King Wally pushed his way past the old woman and entered her house to have a closer look at the statue. The old woman spluttered and stammered at this boy pushing his way into her house.

"What have you done to him? Turn him back!" King Wally demanded.

The old woman, rightfully annoyed, said, "Young man, what is the meaning of this? You get out of my house!"

Some of the kids were too scared to enter the witch's house and stayed outside, while others also pushed their way past the old woman into the house to protect their self-proclaimed king.

Hearing the commotion coming from the other room, Fearless

entered the foyer from the living room and asked, "What's going on?"

King Wally and the other kids stared at Fearless.

"I don't know what is going on. Do you know these children?" the old woman asked.

"Yes, Ms. Wilson. These are my friends," Fearless said. To King Wally, he asked, "What *are* you doing here?"

"What am *I* doing here?" King Wally asked, "What are *you* doing here? How do you know her name? And, what did she do to this boy?" King Wally patted the statue on the head.

"I'm here to help Ms. Wilson with her backyard. I know her name, because I introduced myself when I came over to get the ball the other day. She asked me to mow her lawn. A family of rabbits lives in her backyard and she was afraid snakes might get them if the grass grows too tall. As for that boy, Ms. Wilson made that sculpture of her grandson."

"Oh," King Wally said, and lowered his head.

"You should not enter people's backyards or houses without asking for permission first. And, you shouldn't break people's things, like the sculpture of Ms. Wilson's dog you broke. You should show more respect, to both people and boundaries," Fearless said. King Wally lowered his head further in embarrassment.

"I'm sorry, Ms. Wilson," King Wally said. The other kids apologized, too, as they left the house and returned to the empty lot.

"Sorry about my friends. And, I'm sorry he broke your dog," Fearless said.

"No need to apologize," Ms. Wilson said. "I can always make another one."

Fearless invited Ms. Wilson to watch the kids play kickball. She appreciated the offer and enjoyed watching the kids play. King Wally, who still felt bad, kept a lawn chair by the sidewalk for her. Whenever anyone kicked the ball over the fence, she was happy to let them fetch the ball from her yard, as long as they asked permission first.

"Danny, next time, ask Liz before you come into her room and play with her toys," Dad said.

"I did, yesterday. And, I brought it back when I was done. I'm not responsible for her losing things."

"Ok. Good," Dad turned from Danny to Liz, "Do not take something of Danny's without asking."

"But, he—..."

"Elizabeth, do not take other people's things without asking."

"Okay," Liz mumbled. This was not the first time to hear that this week. She turned to Danny and asked, "If you put it back, where is it now?"

"Danny?" Dad asked.

"What? I put it back on her dresser!" Danny said, getting defensive.

"It's not there," Liz said with the tone of accusation still in her voice.

Dad walked up to the dresser and looked around. Liz had a lot of things on top of her dresser. He was surprised she could find anything up there.

"Is that it?" Danny asked, pointing to a small bit of string exposed from behind the dresser.

Being careful not to knock anything off, Dad pulled the dresser out a bit to reach the string. Dad dangled the string with the button at the end in front of Liz. Her lost button-yoyo must have fallen behind the dresser, probably pushed by the other things piled all over the surface.

"You found it!" she said, to Dad.

"Who did?" Danny asked, squinting at Liz.

Dad gave her a look. As she took her yoyo, she turned to Danny and said, "Sorry, Danny. Thank you for finding it."

Liz hugged Danny. When she was finished, she said, "Now,

get out of my room.''

The Sound of Courage

A story about standing up

for one's personal beliefs and opinions.

Just before bedtime, after Danny had put on his jammies and brushed his teeth, he snuck to his school backpack, riffled through the contents, found the book he was looking for and quickly headed back to his bedroom as quiet as a ninja. When he saw Dad look up from his computer at him, he said, "Just grabbing my library book," and rushed towards his room with the book hugged tightly to his chest. Passing the bathroom where Liz had finished brushing her teeth, Danny tripped and his book tumbled out of his arms and skidded to a halt in front of Liz. She bent down to pick up the book for Danny.

"May I have my book?" Danny asked, holding out his hand.

"You're reading this?" Liz scoffed.

"Just give it back," he said. He pulled the book out of Liz's hand.

"That book is for little kids, like me," Liz said, giggling.

By the time Dad arrived on the scene, Danny had hidden his book under his pillow while Liz teased him about it. Danny's face turned bright red with embarrassment.

"Dad, tell Liz to stop teasing me," Danny said.

"Liz, stop teasing your brother."

"I just think it's funny Danny's reading Puppy Princess," Liz said.

"Liz, it is a good thing when Danny reads any book, so we shouldn't discourage that."

"Even if it's Puppy Princess?" Liz teased.

"Dad!"

"Elizabeth, enough. And, yes, even if he is reading Puppy Princess," Dad said to Liz, and then turned to Danny and asked, "What is Puppy Princess?"

"I don't want to talk about it. It's too embarrassing," Danny mumbled.

"Don't let other people make you feel embarrassed about things you like. Be like Charlie. Stand up for what you believe in."

"Charlie?" Danny asked, confused. He then realized Dad was about to tell him another story.

THE SOUND OF COURAGE

Charlie was in fifth grade. At the end of the year, the school required all fifth graders to perform in a talent show. Kids could sing, dance, play an instrument, juggle, act, or any number of other creative performances. Some kids also contributed art exhibits, like drawings, paintings, sculptures, or framed poems to the art show and silent auction fundraiser. Charlie did not know if his talent was good enough for the talent show. He had a talent for mimicking sounds.

His dad wanted Charlie to be a sports hero. His mom encouraged him to become more involved in the arts. Charlie was not athletic, and often very clumsy. And, even though he could imitate all kinds of sounds, Charlie couldn't carry a tune and could only draw stick figure people and animals.

His parents asked him what he wanted to do for the talent show. Although Charlie played some basketball with his dad, he wasn't extremely talented at it. He couldn't dance or sing. Charlie knew his real talent was making sounds, but he was too nervous to tell his parents. Instead, he told his parents he still had to think about it.

As the end of the school year approached, they asked him every day if he knew what to do for the talent show. As the days passed and the talent show drew nearer, he finally told his parents about his talent for making sounds. A good parent would support their child, help them practice, and fill them with encouragement. Charlie's parents were good parents, but they thought he was joking. They laughed and said making sounds seemed childish, and not much of a talent. Hearing this, he felt embarrassed about his talent for making sounds, even in front of his parents. He wanted to prove to his mom and dad he could make sounds, but they made him nervous and the sounds he demonstrated to them weren't his best. His parents were not impressed and suggested he think of another talent for the show.

Instead of auditions, the fifth grade teachers asked each student to demonstrate their talent for the rest of the class. On Charlie's turn, he felt more nervous than when he tried to make sounds for his parents. Plus, he had never made sounds at school in front of his friends. Usually, he imitated sounds when no one else was around.

When he told his teacher he could make sounds for his talent, the only thing she said was, "Huh. Ok."

Some of the students rolled their eyes and shook their heads. Charlie grew more nervous. He thought of a couple of his favorite and best sounds he liked to make, but when he tried to make them, they sounded nothing like he intended them. When he asked to try again, his teacher made a comment about him having some more time to practice before the show. Even though the teacher meant no harm by her comment, some of the kids laughed. This embarrassed Charlie. He returned to his seat with his bright red face and broken sounds.

As the show drew nearer, Charlie became more nervous and shy about making sounds. When the word of his talent spread around the school, other kids asked him to make different noises. When he refused to makes sounds on demand, they scoffed and laughed at him. Even when he practiced alone, he began to doubt himself and wondered why he thought he was any good. Making different sounds wasn't what it used to be. He did not want to be in the talent show anymore, but knew he had to since it was part of his participation and presentation grades.

A week before the talent show, a new student transferred to Charlie's class from a different school. She was a cute girl named Samantha who couldn't speak. It was not because she was shy or deaf. Samantha was mute. Samantha was in an accident when she was just a little baby. Because of the accident, her tongue and vocal chords had never developed properly and she had never been able to speak. She learned to speak through sign language and could write in neat, pretty handwriting. To talk with the other children in class who didn't know sign language, she carried around a small whiteboard with a pen, wrote out her words, and held up the sign like a cartoon speech bubble.

The other kids were shy and didn't know what to say to Samantha. Charlie was fascinated by her and was the first child in class to introduce himself to her. She asked Charlie about his talent. Charlie felt more embarrassed and didn't feel like sharing. Here was a girl who couldn't speak or make much noise at all, and his talent was making sounds. Charlie wondered if his talent would embarrass her or if she would take it the wrong way and think he was making fun of her.

When he told her, she was delighted! She told him she loved listening to different sounds. When Charlie asked about Samantha's talent, she pulled a photo album out of her school bag. She showed him pictures of her talent—making puppets. Charlie wondered how she could put on a puppet show without speaking. He had an idea.

Together, he and Samantha asked their teacher if they could put on a puppet show together for the talent show. Samantha could work the puppets and Charlie could be her voice. Their teacher agreed they could team up for the talent show, on the condition that Charlie would need to display his talent for making sounds and not just provide voices for the people puppets. He agreed.

On the day of the show, Charlie was still very nervous. Samantha assured him everything would be okay. When it was time for their act, he helped Samantha set everything up. She had a white sheet held up on a frame and positioned a light to shine upon the sheet from behind. Samantha sat on the floor with her puppets while Charlie sat to the side in a chair with a microphone. Where he sat, he couldn't even see the audience, only Samantha, her puppets, and the shadows displayed on the sheet.

At first, Charlie's nervousness caused him to make one of the sounds too loud into the microphone so that it caused squealing feedback. He adjusted the volume of his voice and the distance between his mouth and the microphone. As the puppet show progressed, he became more and more comfortable and confident making his sounds. The birds twittered. The unicorn neighed. The dragon roared. And, his sounds brought more life to Samantha's shadows on the sheet. The audience clapped and cheered in all the right places. And, when Charlie and Samantha were done, they stood in front of the curtain and bowed to a standing ovation.

After the show, everyone congratulated them on their amazing performance. The other kids wanted Charlie to teach them how to make such marvelous sounds, and asked Samantha how she was able to make such lifelike shadow puppets. Charlie's parents were impressed with the sounds he made. The teacher gave both of them A's for their performance. From that moment on, Charlie was no longer nervous about his unique talent, and proudly shared it with anyone who would ask.

"You see? People expected Charlie to do one thing, but he wanted to do something different that was unique to him. Don't listen to people who think what you're reading isn't for you and think you should be reading something else. I'm thrilled you found a book you enjoy reading."

"Thanks, Dad," Danny said, and gave his dad a hug. "I liked your story."

"So, what is Puppy Princess?" Dad asked.

Before Danny could answer, Liz said, "It's this cartoon on TV. Something about a dog protecting her castle from evil cats."

"Do you watch the show?" Dad asked Liz.

Liz shrugged, "Just the commercials."

"Do you watch the show, Danny?" he asked. Danny nodded, blushing.

"And, because you like the show, you wanted to read the book?"

He nodded again.

"Why do you like it?" Dad asked.

Danny shrugged and said, "I know it's a show for little kids and it's kind of girly, but it makes me laugh. And, I think the animation is awesome. Oh, and the world is really cool, too. Magic everywhere!" The more Danny talked about the show, the more animated he became. He made it clear how much he liked it.

"That's cool. Thanks for sharing," Dad said. "Do you think I would like it?"

"I don't know, Dad. You might be way too old for it," Danny said.

"Maybe I could watch it with you sometime," he said, sounding more like a question or a suggestion. Danny blushed, again.

"I didn't know about all that other stuff. I only knew about

the stuff from the commercials. Can I watch it with you, too?"
Liz asked.

"Sure," Danny said. "You can laugh at the funny parts, but no asking questions or talking until the commercials."

The Life of Lies

A story about lying.

Liz and Danny worked on their homework, while Dad joined them at the table with his laptop. For several minutes, the only sounds were Dad's tapping of keys, the scratching of pencils, and Liz's swinging feet kicking the legs of her chair.

Dad broke the peaceful moment by asking, "Hey, Danny, do you know how you did on your science test?"

Danny hung his head and said, "Yeah. I got a C."

"Next time, if you study, I bet you can get an A or a B. What about that homework assignment? Did you talk to your teacher?"

"Yeah. She said there was a mix up in the office. The wrong copies were placed in her box. We worked on the actual assignment in class."

Dad nodded and returned his attention back to his computer. Less than a minute later, he looked up and asked, "Liz, did anything...interesting happen at school today?"

Liz continued to work on her homework, and without looking up, said, "Nope."

"Are you sure?" Dad asked.

Liz sunk lower in her chair, didn't look up, but shook her head and said, "Nothing I can think of."

"Let me ask you another question. Do you know anything about some trampled flowers?" Dad asked.

"I don't know. Some kids were playing in the flower bed," Liz said, quietly.

"So, you do know something. Do you know any of the kids?"

Liz shook her head, but still didn't look at her dad.

"Liz? Look at me, and tell me you don't know any of the kids," Dad said.

Liz raised her head. Tears rolled down her cheeks.

"That was you?!" Danny said, shocked.

"Do you want to change your answer?" Dad asked. He swiveled his laptop around. On the screen was a snippet of video captured by one the school's security cameras of five girls running and playing in one of the flower beds, trampling the violets under their child-sized shoes. One of the girls looked like a slightly blurred version of Liz.

"That was you!" Danny said, and laughed.

Dad gave Danny a warning glance. Danny stopped laughing, mouthed "Sorry," and returned to his homework.

"You and your friends did trample the flowers, didn't you?"

Frowning and sobbing, she nodded.

"Liz, why did you lie to me?"

Liz slouched in her chair and shrugged. "I was afraid."

"You were afraid of getting into trouble?"

"No, well, yes, but I'm afraid Mommy doesn't want to come home."

Dad looked confused. "Mommy is coming back tonight. What does that have to do with you not telling me about the flowers?"

"I don't know," Liz squeaked. She cleared her throat, sat up a little straighter, and said, "We were having too much fun. And, we ran through the flowers on accident. I didn't know it was wrong until the teacher yelled at us. While we were sitting in time out, I thought about Mommy. What if she's having too much fun on her trip and forgets to come home."

"Ah. Thank you for clearing that up. Mommy won't forget to come home. I know she misses us very much and probably can't wait to be home. Okay?"

Liz nodded.

"Still...Even though you are worried about Mommy, that's no reason to lie to me and hide what really happened."

Liz nodded, again.

"We encourage you to tell us the truth. I remember a time I lied to your Granny and Grandpa. I didn't want to get in trouble. My lies took on a life of their own."

THE LIFE OF LIES

When I was a kid, my parents sent me to a house down the street to bring home a plastic punch bowl the neighbors had borrowed. I was not watching where I was going, and I tripped over a crack in the sidewalk. I was okay, but the punch bowl tumbled out of my hands and broke in two when it hit the sidewalk. I felt like an idiot tripping over such a shallow crack. I'm glad it wasn't their nicer, glass punch bowl. Unfortunately, I knew my parents needed the punch bowl for an upcoming bridge party. I was terrified what my parents would do when they found out I broke it. My parents were nice, but I still imagined all sorts of terrible punishments for breaking it.

I got home and showed them the broken bowl. When they asked what happened, instead of admitting I was a klutz and telling them the truth, I told them a lie about a bully knocking the bowl out of my hands which caused it to break.

"I'm glad the bully didn't hurt you," my mom said.

"Watch out for bullies, because they tend to do things like that," my dad warned.

I felt guilty about lying to my parents. It made me feel worse they believed my lie. I needed to do something to repay them for the broken punch bowl, but I didn't have much money and didn't know how I could earn more.

The next day, I played down the street at my friend's house. On my way home, a kid I had never seen before stopped me. He was bigger and stronger than me. He chewed on the wooden end of a matchstick, which made him look even tougher. I had never met the kid before, but he seemed to know me.

"Hey kid," he said to me, "Look, I'm sorry I knocked that bowl outta your hands yesterday. That wasn't right, an' I feel bad."

"Uh. Okay," I said. He didn't knock the punch bowl out of my hands. I tripped. He apologized for what I had lied to my parents about.

"Look, take this money. I wanna repay you for what I broke.

Should be enough," he said. He grabbed my wrist in a firm grip and slapped a folded stack of bills into my hand.

"I can't take your money," I said. I didn't know how he got that much money, which was more than enough to replace the broken bowl. He did not need to give me money for being a klutz and lying. I wondered how many kids he may have bullied for that much lunch money.

"No, I want you to have it," he said, and closed my fingers around the wad of cash. "Look, I do a lot of mean things, but I'm not a mean person. I do mean things because I want to seem like I'm tough. I won the money winning a poetry contest. And, if you even start to laugh about that, I'll beat the snot outta you. I write poetry to help express the feelings I'm too embarrassed to show. I'm sorry for breaking your bowl. I want you to use the money to buy yourself a new one. Got it?"

I didn't know what happened. I didn't know how to earn enough money to repay my parents, but here was a stranger giving me plenty of money to buy a new punch bowl that he took the blame for breaking and felt sorry about something he didn't even do. I nodded, as if I understood, even though I didn't.

Satisfied he repaid me for something he didn't do, the stranger left. Stunned at what had just happened, I still had his money clutched in my hand. How was I going to explain to my parents where all this money came from?

When I got home, I gave my parents the money and apologized for breaking their punch bowl.

"You don't have to apologize for something you didn't do, but thank you," my mom said.

"That's a lot of money," my dad said. "Where did you get it?"

Knowing I shouldn't take things from strangers, I couldn't tell my parents I got the money from one. Instead, I blurted out, "A poetry contest."

My mom's eyes lit up, and she exclaimed, "I didn't know you wrote poetry! Can I hear what you wrote?"

My mom could not contain her excitement, and I could not disappoint her. I don't know what made me do it, but I lied—again. This time, I took the bully's story about the poetry contest, and added a few extra details to make it my own. I told her I couldn't remember exactly what I wrote, but I claimed it was about a tough guy who had trouble expressing his feelings, so he expressed them through poetry. Even though she didn't hear me recite any poem, my parents felt proud of me and thought I was very creative. I had repaid them for the punch bowl and hoped the matter was settled. But, I felt guilty about lying to them—again.

The next day, I got off the school bus on the corner and walked down the street to my house. The bully appeared again, and this time he had somebody with him. The person with him held a notepad and pencil in his hands.

"Look," the bully said pointing at me, "That's the kid who won the poetry contest. He lives on my block!"

"Hi. Gerald Montgomery, here," the bully's friend said, "I work for the local newspaper. Tell me about the poem that won the Young Poets of America contest."

Once again, my lying took on a life of its own. The bully who gave me the money was there. I was afraid if I told the reporter his story, I'd get the snot beaten out of me.

"He's the one who wrote the poem, not me," I said, pointing to the bully.

"Fascinating," the reporter said, "You entered his poem in the contest as your own?"

"You took one of my poems without asking?!" the bully asked, cracking his knuckles in a threatening way.

Before I could explain, the reporter said, "Ah! So, you plagiarized it. You *stole* his poem and entered it as your own. What did you do with the winnings?"

"He gave me the money to repay my parents for the broken punch bowl," I said.

"You took my money, too? I oughta beat the snot out of you!"

the bully said, outraged.

Before I could explain again, the reporter said, "Ah! So you stole his poem and his money. And, you said you squandered it away on fruit punch and bowling?"

I didn't know what was happening. People accused me of all sorts of ridiculous things. I didn't want the snot beaten out of me. I didn't say anything else and ran straight home.

Frightened and guilty, I confessed everything to my parents. I told them how I tripped over a crack in the sidewalk and dropped their punch bowl. I told them how I took the money from a stranger who took the blame for breaking the punch bowl. I told them I never entered a poetry contest. I apologized for lying to them and begged them for forgiveness.

"Oh, we know what you did," my dad said. He showed me page three of the evening newspaper. On the page, there was a picture of me walking down our street after school and an article about me plagiarizing someone else's poem in order to win a poetry contest.

"That never really happened," I said.

"Lying? Cheating? Stealing? I don't know what to believe anymore," my mom said, sobbing into a tissue.

Seeing how much my lies upset my parents taught me a tough lesson. It would have been so much easier if I had told them the truth in the first place. Sometimes lies take on a life of their own. When they do, it's hard to rebuild trust with the people lied to.

"Daddy, did that really happen?" Liz asked.

He shrugged and said, "It might be the truth, it might be a lie. You see? When people tell lies, it's sometimes hard to tell the difference between what's real and what's not. The truth has ways of revealing itself. You made a bad decision, and you and your friends got yourselves in trouble. Your principal sent this email and has asked the parents of the children in the video to help replace the flowers. This weekend, we are going to buy some new flowers and replant the ones you and your friends trampled."

"Really?" she asked, sitting up straighter in the chair.

"Yes," Dad said, "But, because you didn't tell me what happened when I asked, I'm taking away screen time for a few days."

She groaned.

"That means no TV until after this weekend. Especially, not until you have helped replant the flowers. Since I will need to help you with the school's flowerbed on Saturday, you can help me destroy other plants by pulling weeds on Sunday."

She groaned louder, and sniffled.

"Blow your nose. Finish your homework. Ok?"

Liz nodded as she walked away to get a tissue.

Trust One Another

A story about supporting other people.

"Yellow. Yellow. Yellow," Liz whispered to herself. She looked at the remaining few crayons in the box and under a few crumpled pieces of paper. Not finding her yellow crayon, she grabbed the purple one instead and began drawing on the blank side of an advertisement flyer. Whenever flyers appeared on their front door, they often became scratch paper for Liz's artwork.

"Dinner's almost ready," Dad announced, then to Danny he said, "Danny, do you mind setting the table?"

"Yeah, okay." Danny grabbed the stack of plates and pulled three forks from the drawer.

Danny froze as he approached the dinner table. The fallout from Liz and her coloring claimed most of the space where Danny needed to set the table. Her other drawings and the crayons lay scattered across the length of the table. Some crayons had rolled outward from where she sat towards all corners and edges of the table.

"Uh, Dad?" Danny called.

Dad poked his head out of the kitchen to survey Liz's mess. "Liz, can you clear some room so we can eat?"

"I'm trying to finish a picture for Mommy," Liz said, not looking up from her scribbling.

"Danny, try to work around the mess," Dad said, and then disappeared into the kitchen.

"If Mom were here, she'd tell Liz to clean up her mess," Danny muttered.

Dad returned with a pot of cooked spaghetti and a bowl of sliced Italian sausage. "Mom is not here, but she will be back later tonight. For now, just work around your sister and her mess." He cleared a couple of spaces to set down the pot and bowl. The oven buzzer for the garlic bread called him back to the kitchen.

"When will Mommy be back?" Liz asked, still coloring.

"Late."

"Why did she have to go out of town?" Danny asked, following his dad's lead and shoving paper and crayons aside to be able to set the table for dinner.

"She is training for her new job."

"Why did Mommy start a new job?" Liz asked.

Before Dad could respond, Danny added, "Why did Dad start telling us crazy stories?"

"Daddy, are you going to tell us crazy stories after Mommy gets back?" Liz asked.

Dad brought a plate of buttery garlic bread and a small saucepan of spaghetti sauce from the kitchen and set them on the table, "Those are all great questions." He went to kitchen, and returned a moment later with three glasses of water.

As Dad took a seat at the table, he picked up Liz's plate to serve her some plain spaghetti noodles with a side of sausage and a slice of garlic bread. He then, fixed his own plate.

"Mommy started a new job, because you are older now and in school. Sometimes, Mom and I do things without explanation, and we do not always explain why. I started telling you crazy stories while Mom is out of town to help teach you in a way, hopefully, you will remember later."

"Like remembering to try new foods, like the Jones family?" Liz asked.

"Or following rules, like Mr. Witherspoon singing at the dinner table?" Danny asked.

"Yes, exactly," Dad said. "Thank you for listening to my crazy stories. I may not be able to clearly explain the reasons for what Mom and I tell you, like why Mom started a new job. Mom's job is important to her, and we should support what is important to her, just like Puppy Princess is important to Danny, or setting the table around Liz's mess so she can reach a good stopping

point on her drawing before dinner."

"Or, listening to your crazy stories?" Danny asked.

"Yes, like that."

"Do you have a crazy story about supporting the family?" Danny asked.

TRUST ONE ANOTHER

Once upon a time, in a far away kingdom, the royal family prepared for the departure of the king and queen who were invited to a wedding in a neighboring country.

The king and queen had three children. The king gave each of the royal children a task. Cedric, the elder prince, was left in charge of the kingdom, which was everything from the castle to the kingdom's borders. Victor, the younger prince, was left in charge of the castle and everything within it. Princess Zelda, the youngest of the royal children, was left in charge of her older brothers. The king and queen asked them to trust their parents' wishes and to trust the judgement of each other.

Soon after the departure of the king and queen, trouble brewed in the kingdom and castle. The ogres of the woodlands took the king and queen's absence as an opportunity to attack. The ghosts of the castle took the king and queen's absence to haunt the castle more than usual. The princes had two big problems to face, but neither knew what to do.

Cedric regularly trained with members of the royal guard, and often visited with the kingdom's citizens. He knew they would do anything to defend the kingdom, but Cedric had very little experience with leading an army, especially into a war with the ogres.

Victor had explored every inch of the castle, including all the rooms, corridors, staircases and secret passageways. He encountered many ghosts during his exploration, but was not prepared to handle a massive haunting.

Although the princes did not show it, young Zelda could sense her brothers' concerns. She knew how smart and brave her brothers could be. She also knew exactly how to help them with their problems. She worried they might not go along with her plan.

"Cedric," Zelda said, "Round up the kingdom's farmers and ask each to bring a shovel."

"Farmers? Shovels?" Cedric asked. "I cannot ask farmers to fight with shovels when the royal guard is better trained to defend the kingdom with swords and bows."

"Father asked you to trust me," Zelda said, firmly.

Cedric drew a deep breath, nodded, and left at once to gather farmers with shovels.

"Victor," Zelda said, "Gather all the nuts, berries, and seeds from the kitchen."

"But, Zelda, as hungry as I am, a belly full of nuts and berries will not calm the ghosts. Perhaps I should fetch the village clergy, instead."

"Father asked you to trust me, too," Zelda said. "Bring the nuts and berries to the courtyard, where we will meet our brother when he returns."

"Where are you going, Zelda?" Victor asked.

"I must visit the castle tailors. See you in the courtyard, my brother."

Victor scratched his head. He did not know how nuts and berries would stop the haunting. Nor did he understand why his sister needed the tailors. She often consulted the tailors for making fancy dresses or costumes for plays. Victor could not understand how this would help either situation. Perhaps she called on the tailors to help Cedric's army protect themselves in a fight against the ogres. Father asked him to trust his brother and sister. Cedric left without questioning her. Still puzzled by his sister's requests, he put his trust in her and headed towards the kitchen.

When Victor arrived in the courtyard with three members of the kitchen staff and several crates of nuts and berries, Zelda sat with two of the castle tailors working on what looked like mittens. The tailors had brought a couple rolls of old, grey fabric, scissors, and a few balls of yarn. However, the princess and tailors were not making mittens—they made several hastily crafted pouches. Victor wondered if the pouches were to contain a mix of the nuts and berries to feed the soldiers. He still had no idea how this would help dispel the castle ghosts nor defend the castle from woodland ogres.

Zelda and the tailors had finished making several pouches by the time Cedric returned with six of the kingdom's farmers, each carrying a shovel over their shoulder. Cedric himself carried two spare shovels, in case he and his brother needed them for Zelda's plan.

"Wonderful, my brothers. You have done well. Everyone, help fill these pouches with a scoop of dirt from the courtyard. Use the yarn to tie the pouch tight so that no dirt spills out. When you are done, please bring them to me," Zelda said.

The brothers and farmers used the shovels to churn up the dirt from the courtyard and scoop a small pile into each of the small pouches. The tailors checked the knots on each of the pouches to ensure they were closed tight. Soon, several dirt-filled pouches sat in a small mound at Zelda's feet.

Zelda placed the pouches randomly around the courtyard, while the kitchen staff followed behind her surrounding each pouch with a ring of nuts, berries, and seeds. When she finished setting out the pouches, she brushed off her hands and said, "There."

"Now what, my sister?" the princes asked.

"We wait."

"For what?" Victor asked, still very confused. The brothers looked at each other and shrugged. Though nothing was said, they continued to trust their sister.

The princes sat with the kitchen staff on the mostly emptied crates. The farmers leaned on their shovels. Everyone looked around the courtyard at the pouches, but were unsure what, if anything, would happen next.

"For that," Zelda said, and pointed to one of the pouches in the courtyard.

Ravens descended into the courtyard, perched upon the pouches, and fed on the nuts and berries. Zelda often bird-watched and knew how much the ravens liked berries and nuts.

One of the farmers gasped and pointed towards one of the ravens close by. The others looked at where he pointed. Like magic, the loose ends of yarn, which had tied the pouches shut, tangled themselves around the raven's talons. The same thing happened for each of the other ravens. One moment, the raven feasted on the ring of treats around the pouch, the next the yarn wove itself around the bird's talons. The ravens cawed at the yarn, then settled to continue feeding on the nuts and berries.

"What sorcery is this?" Victor asked, mesmerized by the pouches tying themselves to ravens.

"The *spooky* kind," Zelda said, wiggling her fingers at her brother and giggling. She winked at her older brother who asked, "Now what?"

"Now, this," she said. She walked to the middle of the courtyard, held her arms high above her head, and announced, "You know what to do! Fly forth!"

The bakers, tailors, farmers, and princes watched all the ravens take flight, carrying the small and mysterious self-tying pouches of dirt with them. The flock flew up and out of the courtyard.

"Come, my brothers! Let us follow!" Zelda said, and ran to the front gates. Outside the castle, the stableboy had three horses prepared for the royal children. Zelda swung herself up onto her horse and galloped in the direction of the flock of ravens still visible in the sky.

"Cedric!" Victor said, "She is heading towards the ogre woods!"

"We must hurry!" Cedric said.

The two princes raced their horses after the princess. They caught up with her at a clearing at the edge of the woods. Ogres emerged from the trees and shook their clubs and grunted threats at the royal children. Looking up, the princes saw the ravens circling the clearing high above. The ogres shook their clubs and grunted at the ravens, too.

Cedric brought his horse to one side of Zelda and Victor trotted up to her other side. In unison, the brothers asked, "Now what?"

"Watch." the princess said, pointing up at the ravens.

Dozens of ogres charged out of the forest towards the royal siblings. The ogres slowed down when they saw ravens descending from above. The ravens swooped lower, yet still out of reach of the ogres and their clubs. The pouches untied themselves from the ravens' talons and dropped to the field with soft thuds. The ravens retreated to the trees, leaving the ogres and pouches behind in the clearing.

The ogres slowed down and scratched their heads. Like the princes, the ogres were clearly confused. They cautiously approached the pouches. The ogres looked down and poked the little pouches with their feet and clubs.

Zelda knew about the castle ghosts and how restless they had grown of being trapped by the castle grounds. She hoped the pouches of dirt would allow them to move beyond the castle walls. Sure enough, one by one, shimmery, blue-green ghosts drifted up from each of the pouches. As the ghosts took a clearer form, they stretched and flexed their see-through arms and legs. The ogres did not trust the ghosts and swung their clubs at them, which did no harm and passed through the ghosts' misty bodies.

Zelda had heard tales of how superstitious ogres could be. If the ravens did not spook the ogres, she hoped the ghosts might. The ghosts waved their arms, made silly faces at the ogres, and moaned, "Boogedy boogedy!" Squealing like pigs, the ogres dropped their clubs and ran as fast as they could back into the woods from which they came.

The royal children laughed all the way back to the castle. Both brothers admired how their sister handled both problems at once. Though they had their doubts about their own abilities and each other, it was clear they performed best when supporting each other's judgement.

Danny and Liz laughed at the thought of ogres running away, squealing like pigs.

"Good one, Dad," Danny said.

"Where do you get these crazy stories?" Liz asked.

With a straight face, Dad said, "Mail order. They leave flyers on our door."

Liz grabbed her drawing and flipped it over. She tilted her head to the side, gave him a look, and said, "Daddy, this is about lawn mowers."

"Not that one. Must have been another flyer," Dad said.

Liz intensified her look.

"What? You don't trust me? Would I lie to you?" Dad said, with a smile and a wink.

"If you're not careful, Dad, your lies will take on a life of their own and become a story about mowing lawns," Danny said.

Changing the subject, Dad asked Liz, "What did you draw for Mom?"

Liz flipped the flyer back to the side with her drawing and proudly showed it to the table.

"You know giraffes aren't purple, right?" Danny asked.

Liz frowned at Danny and said, "I couldn't find the yellow crayon."

With mock shock, Danny said, "What? I'm surprised you couldn't find it under this mess."

"Danny," Dad warned.

"Sorry, Liz," he said to his sister. He turned to his dad and asked, "Do you know any stories about purple giraffes?"

"No, those stories are from the deluxe membership," Dad said with a grin and a wink.

"Well, I do," Liz said. As they finished eating, she proceeded to make up her own crazy story about Yolanda, the purple giraffe of Mars.

Dangerous Distractions

A story about interrupting.

After dinner, Dad sat at his computer. Liz, no longer able to watch TV, sat at the table and colored a picture of an elephant in her coloring book.

Liz looked up from her coloring book and asked, "Dad, when does Mom get home?"

"Late. She'll be home after you go to bed."

"Ok," Liz said, and continued to color.

As Dad started typing again, Liz walked up to Dad, gave him a hug, and asked, "Are you going to tell Mom about the broken mushroom and the flowers?"

"I think it should come from you, but yes, one of us needs to tell her," Dad said.

"Oh," Liz moaned. She let go of Dad and shuffled back to her coloring book.

"Do you like my picture?" Liz said, holding up her coloring book for Dad to see.

"Mm hm. Very nice."

Before Dad could type anything, Danny wandered into the room and asked, "When is Mom coming home?"

"Like I told your sister, she'll be back late, after you are in bed."

"Oh. Ok. What are you working on?" Danny asked.

"Work stuff."

"Looks like you're just sitting there staring at your screen," he said.

"I'm trying to concentrate, but I keep getting interrupted," Dad said.

"Sor-ry," Danny said, offended.

"I'm not fussing at you, I'm just trying to get a thought out of my head, but the interruptions make me lose my concentration. Why don't you and Liz go upstairs and find a game to play?" Dad gave Danny a half hug and then ruffled up his hair.

Danny stepped away and straightened his hair. He walked up to Liz to convince her to abandon her coloring book and go upstairs to play a game. Since she couldn't find the color crayon she wanted for the palm tree, she agreed to play with her brother. They went to Danny's room, where they hoped they wouldn't disturb Dad, but the game they invented did not help.

"What sound does an elephant make?" Liz asked.

Danny imitated a decent elephant noise by buzzing his lips.

"You know what makes this noise?" Danny asked. He made the same elephant noise, only this time he moved his finger up and down over his buzzing lips. "An elephant underwater."

"What about a monkey underwater?" Liz asked.

They both made underwater monkey noises, then broke into raucous laughter.

Danny and Liz thought up weird noises to make and the other tried their best to imitate the noise. From cowboy chickens to monsters eating potato chips, the more ridiculous the suggestion, the harder they laughed. They got so loud, the neighbors could probably hear their noises and laughter all the way down the street. As entertaining as it was for them, their game was more distracting to Dad than the questions they had asked him earlier.

There was a light knock on the door to Danny's room. The noises and laughter stopped. Danny opened the door. "Hey, Dad. Did we disturb you?"

"Yes, a bit. I don't want to break up your fun, but I am trying to finish something. Would you mind taking it down a bit?"

"Sure, Dad."

"Sorry," Liz whispered.

"Thanks," Dad said. He headed back to his computer and Danny closed his door.

Dad knocked on his door again.

Danny answered the door and said, "What? We didn't even make any noise."

"I know," Dad said, "Did I ever tell you the story about with a knight in shining armor and a dragon?"

"No," they both said, with interest.

"Don't you have work to finish?" Danny asked.

"While I'm distracted, I thought I'd tell you this story, because it happens to be about interruptions and distractions."

DANGEROUS DISTRACTIONS

Once upon a time, there was a village with an old storyteller. Long before television and radio, people, especially the children of the village, would gather around the storyteller and listen to him tell stories.

"What kind of story would you like today?" the storyteller asked.

"One with a dragon!"

"And a knight in shining armor!"

"And treasure!"

"Ah," the storyteller said with a smile. "I know just the one. It has a dragon and a knight and treasure. But, it can be a very scary story, and I don't know if you are ready to hear it."

"Is it really scary?"

"Yes!"

"Tell it! Tell it!" the children begged.

"All right, but you must listen and not interrupt this story, because—"

"What if we get scared?"

"You must not interrupt, even if you are scared, because—"

"Why is it important not to interrupt?"

"I'm trying to tell you why, but you keep interrupting, which you must not do, because of...*the dragon*!"

Some kids cuddled up to the bigger kids, already concerned about the dragon. Other kids, especially the boys, grinned and rubbed their hands together, knowing this was going to be a great story. The storyteller began.

* * *

Once upon a time, a faraway kingdom had problems with a terrible dragon. Like most dragons, this dragon loved to take gold coins and gems from the kingdom. The dragon also liked stealing other shiny objects, like mirrors, polished plates, and silverware. This particular dragon liked stealing these things because it loved how the sun reflected off the surface of such shiny objects. It loved catching a glitter and glimmer of light out of the corner of its eye. It loved this sparkle more than feeding on glittering fairies.

"Oh no! Not fairies!" said a little girl.

"Yes, fairies. Now, please, do not interrupt this story," the storyteller said.

The dragon cocked its head to the side and sniffed the air. It responded to the small voice with a low growl. It growled for the same reason it liked shiny, glittering objects, because this was a distraction dragon! Instead of collecting all the shiny objects into one enormous pile in a cave the way other dragons do, the distraction dragon scattered its treasure around so that twinkling lights caught its eye from anywhere and everywhere as the sun or moon light passed over each shiny object.

When a person is distracted from their thoughts, they sometimes get angry, because they lose the thoughts they had been thinking about. A distraction dragon is similar to this, but much more intense. When a distraction dragon is left alone with its thoughts, it begins to think about how good life is and how happy it feels. When it feels happy, it falls asleep. But, not all dragons like being happy. They like stomping around, frightening people, terrorizing villages, and collecting more treasure. What is the point of being a dragon if you cannot be ferocious? When something interrupts these happy thoughts, the loss is replaced with a great, burning anger. And so, the distraction dragon scattered shiny objects around so the glittering lights would distract it from its happy thoughts and it can stomp around and cause lots of trouble.

"Wouldn't a knight in shining armor be a bad thing to save the kingdom?" asked a boy.

"Yes, it would. Now, please, no more interruptions," the storyteller said.

The dragon heard people talking, somewhere. It roared. The people of the kingdom shook with fear and wished for someone to save them. The king sent out five of his best knights in shining armor, but only one of them returned to tell the king they were dealing with a distraction dragon. The other four knights who didn't return had become the dragon's dinner. Their armor was shredded to pieces and sprinkled about to sparkle in the sunlight.

The king offered a reward for anyone who could slay the dragon. The king refused to lose any more of his knights. The people in the kingdom were terrified at the thought of fighting a dragon. Only one man wearing a dark, grey cloak and carrying a tall, wooden walking stick went before the king and said he would handle of the dragon.

The king said, "Although your cloak is thick, it will be little protection from the dragon's sharp teeth and fiery breath."

"My cloak will be fine," the man said.

"How do you intend to kill the dragon? I am told shining swords make the dragon more ferocious. A wooden stick, although it does not shine like a sword, is no match for a dragon's thick, scaly hide."

"There are other ways of handling dragons," the man said.

"Then, go forth with your mysterious ways. If you defeat the dragon and return, the reward is yours," the king proclaimed.

The man bowed to the king and left to defeat the dragon. He walked out of the castle, over the fields and hills, and through the forest to find the dragon.

"How can he beat the dragon with a cloak and stick?" a boy asked.

"I bet it's a cloak of invisibility," said another boy.

"And, the stick is a magic wand," said a girl.

"And, I asked you not to interrupt the story. Otherwise, it will hear you," the storyteller said.

"What will hear us?" another girl asked.

"Why, the distraction dragon, of course!" the storyteller said. The children looked at each other. Some shook their heads as if the storyteller was joking, but others looked scared because they had the feeling this was no joke. The storyteller asked, "Now, where was I?"

"Now, where am I?" asked the man to himself. He knew the best way to find a distraction dragon was to wander around daydreaming, and have something distract his thoughts. He also knew that was also the way to get caught off guard by a distraction dragon.

Something shiny caught his eye. On the ground, a few feet away, lay a single, polished coin. The man thought, "Ah, I must be getting close."

He walked carefully and quietly through the meadow. He spotted more and more shiny objects scattered in the grass and knew he must be getting very close to the dragon's lair.

The man looked around. Shiny objects speckled the forest. There were too many items to pick up, especially picking up enough before the dragon caught him messing with its treasure.

The man took his staff of wood and stuck it into the ground. He walked through the grass in a wide circle around the staff. Each time he found a shiny object, he positioned it so the reflected sunlight shone towards the top of his staff. When enough shiny objects shone towards the staff, he pulled out a polished crystal and attached it to the top. The reflected sunlight hit the crystal and split into hundreds of little rainbows all over the ground, the rocks, the trees, and every surface of the dragon's lair.

The man stood back to admire his work. The ground shook as several, heavy footsteps pounded in his direction. The man crouched down and covered himself with the cloak. He had covered himself just in time when the dragon crashed into the field and saw hundreds of little rainbows on everything. The dragon traced the rainbows back to the stick with the crystal at the top. It let out a mighty roar that shook the trees.

"Oh no! Watch out!" the kids said.

"Silence, or it will hear you," the storyteller hissed at the kids, and then stopped. He whispered, "Too late. It has already heard you."

The dragon heard children interrupting a storyteller's story. The air above the storyteller churned like smoke caught in a breeze. The branches of the trees above the storyteller blurred and blended as if they were painted, but then smeared together. Two scaly, reptilian hands with sharp talons clawed at the swirl of color above him, and the colors mixed and blended some more. The dragon's claws scratched and swiped at the storyteller's imagination above his head, fighting its way to get out, but this fight was like trying to fan away a dense fog. An eye of the dragon peeked through the swirl of the storyteller's imagination and spied the terrified children listening to his story. The children were too scared to speak or move.

The dragon roared and continued scratching its way out of the storyteller's imagination. The children shook with fear and stared at the claws ripping at the air.

"The dragon is right above my head trying to get out of my story, isn't it?" the storyteller asked quietly and calmly.

The children nodded, looking between the dragon's claws and the storyteller.

"Everything will be okay if you concentrate on me and let me finish my story. Okay?" he said, calmly.

The children nodded, again.

"All eyes on me. Listen to my voice. Ready? Good."

The man in the cloak knew something had distracted the dragon from his rainbow trap. The dragon clawed at something the man could not see. In its clawing and scratching, it knocked over the stick with the crystal. Whatever had distracted the dragon more than his rainbows held the dragon's attention. He could work with this new distraction.

As quiet as a shadow, the man removed his cloak and crept towards the dragon. The dragon continued to claw at the air. A swirl of colors hovered in the air in front of the dragon. The man did not understand at first, but he thought he saw children's faces in the swirls of colors. He ignored the swirl of colors and the faces. He needed to concentrate in order to take care of the distraction dragon.

In one swift movement, the man swept his cloak over the dragon's head and tied it as fast as he could under the dragon's chin. The man leapt to safety just in time before the dragon snapped his head around and roared, but its mighty roar turned into a mighty yawn. Its arms were not long enough to reach under its chin, and it could not swivel its long neck into a position where its claws could reach. The dragon shook its head from side to side to loosen the cloak, but the man had tied it very tight. The dragon yawned again. Its body crashed to the ground and its breathing slowed. The swirl of colors above the dragon slowly faded away.

The man knew the best way to defeat a distraction dragon was to take away its distractions. The prism on his walking stick was meant o capture the dragon's attention, but the swirl of colors with glimpses of children's faces worked just as well. It would have taken far too long to gather all the shiny objects, but a cloak around its head could both blindfold the dragon's eyes and muffle its ears. With the distractions gone, the dragon started thinking happy thoughts and settled down. Because this dragon had been rampaging for so long, it didn't realize how tired it felt. The dragon drifted into a deep sleep.

With the dragon pacified, the man returned to the king and told him where the dragon could be found. Because the man didn't kill the dragon and only put it to sleep, the king gave the man only half the reward, while the other half paid for a distraction free barn to be built around the dragon to keep it asleep. Half the reward was still more than enough for the man. As long as the cloak stayed around the dragon's head, it would continue to sleep in peace as the kingdom constructed its new home around it.

"And, everyone, including the dragon and the fairies, lived

happily ever after," the storyteller said.

Normally, the children cheered and clapped for the storyteller when he finished one of his stories. Today, they went home to hug their mommies and daddies. From that moment on, before interrupting anyone, they stopped to consider whether what they had to say was worth disturbing a dragon.

"Whoa," Danny said.

"Sorry for bothering you," Liz said.

"Yeah. Sorry to disturb your work," Danny said.

"That's okay. Give me five more minutes to get a few more thoughts out of my head and the three of us can play a game before bedtime," Dad suggested.

Liz and Danny liked the suggestion. They went to the cabinet to find a good game to play, while Dad returned to his computer and jotted down a few notes so he would know where to continue at a later time.

The kids settled on a game of Liar, but needed Dad's help shuffling the cards. Instead of interrupting him, they patiently and quietly built card houses while they waited. When Dad was ready, he joined them at the table, showed them how to shuffle a deck of cards, and played Liar until bedtime.

A Monstrous Mess

A story about cleaning up.

They played a great game of Liar. Danny won telling the truth playing his last card. Both kids thought Dad was a terrible liar.

"Do you think Dad is really bad at lying, or was he letting one of us win?" Danny asked.

"Maybe he's really good at pretending to be really bad at lying," Liz suggested.

"Or, maybe he just didn't have good cards," Dad said, "Do you mind helping clean up? I'd like you to put away your toys."

Danny and Liz grumbled and groaned.

"You do know Mom is coming home tonight. I know you know, because you've asked about a hundred times," Dad said.

"Daddy," Liz said, giving him a look, "We didn't ask you a hundred times."

"Okay. It was more like twice—each. Still, I don't want Mom coming home to a messy house," Dad said.

Danny looked for the mess Dad mentioned. He saw several dishes piled in the sink. The waffle iron sat nestled among the dirty dishes on the counter. The bottle of wood glue also sat on the kitchen counter, waiting patiently to be returned to its shelf in the garage. The toy he and Liz had fought over had found its way to the coffee table. So did the foam apple that had knocked down the block castle. Liz's crayons and coloring books lay scattered throughout the downstairs like Easter eggs, especially around the dinner table. Dad gathered the playing cards used in their game of Liar from the dinner table. Danny knew, even the upstairs playroom had toys ejected from the toy box and littered around the room, plus the wooden blocks, plus more of Liz's coloring books and pages.

Danny agreed—the house was messy.

"We'll help you, Dad," Danny said.

"But, only if you tell us another story while we clean up,"

Liz added.

Danny nodded in agreement.

"What about telling stories at bedtime?"

"Dad," Danny said, "It is bedtime."

"But, you can still tell us a story now, while we help you clean up," Liz added.

So, Dad told a story of a messy house while they tidied up their own house.

A MONSTROUS MESS

Everyone knows the only way a vampire can get into your house is to invite one inside. What people don't realize, this is true for most monsters, not just vampires. Most people do not willingly invite monsters into their home, but they accidentally welcome monsters into their homes all the time. Usually, kids accidentally invite the monsters.

When a child fears a monster in a place where a monster is not, like under the bed, behind the door, or in the closet, monsters take this as an invitation. If a monster is expected to be in places like under the bed, behind the door, or in the closet, the monster feels it is their responsibility to be there. At the earliest opportunity, the monster will accept the invitation and make its way to where they are expected to be. Unfortunately, once a monster is invited into a house, it can be difficult to *un*-invite it. This is important to know for the story I am about to tell you.

Once upon a time, a mother and father decided today was a good day to clean up the basement. They asked their kids to help, but the kids were too afraid to go into the basement. They believed a monster lurked in that dark, musty basement. A tall, lumpy, purple monster wandering down the sidewalk sniffed the air and could smell the children's fear. It accepted their fear as an invitation to live in their basement. It waited patiently behind a tree in the yard for someone to let it inside. The parents spent one weekend cleaning out the basement. When cleaning got too dusty, they opened a window to vent the air. With the window open and while no one was watching, the monster slipped into the basement and made itself at home.

"Mom and I are done cleaning that monstrous mess in the basement, and to celebrate, we are going out for dinner and a movie," the father said.

"Please, do not make any monster-sized messes while we are out," the mother added.

"We won't," the kids said.

After their parents left, the monster came upstairs from the basement. The monster noticed the kids had left their rooms messy, and had not put away their toys in the living room. Because the kids promised not to make a monster-sized mess, the monster figured it was up to the only monster in the house to make the mess instead.

The monster fixed a meal in the kitchen, leaving a sink full of dirty dishes. Then, it dumped the books from the shelves trying to find a scary story, then failed to put back the ones it did not want to read. With a good, scary book and a full belly, the monster returned to the basement. When the parents came home, they were shocked to see the huge mess. They punished the kids.

"It wasn't us! A monster came out of the basement and made this mess," one of the kids claimed.

"I think it was more than one little monster that made this mess," their father said, implying both kids contributed to making the huge mess.

Since their father said more than one monster made the mess, the monster in the basement took that as permission to invite over some of its monster friends. The tall, lumpy, purple monster invited over a sticky, green monster and a fury, red monster with tiny wings.

The next morning, the parents went to work and the kids went to school. While the family was away, the monster in the basement welcomed its friends into the house to play and made an even bigger mess. Since it was too sunny outside, they played hide-n-seek inside. Most of the furniture got rearranged, and everything got thrown out of the closets, cupboards, and drawers to make good hiding places. When the kids arrived home from school, they were shocked to find a bigger mess. They knew if it didn't get it cleaned up, they would be in bigger trouble when their parents got home. Unfortunately, the three monsters made a mess much too big for the kids to clean up, and the kids got in more trouble.

As the kids cleaned the house, their mother said, "This is ridiculous. I can't imagine a bigger mess than this."

The monsters took that as both permission to invite over more monster friends—and as a challenge.

The next day, while the kids were at school and the parents were at work, the monsters invited over all their friends and threw a monster-sized monster party at the house. The tall, lumpy, purple monster welcomed his monster friends of all sizes, colors, textures, and smells into the house for the party. When the kids arrived home from school, the entire house was a mess. Clothes had been thrown all over the place. Food stains splattered the floors, walls, and ceiling. The sofa cushions lay scattered all around. The bedsheets had been tossed around, and in one bedroom, the mattress somehow was caught in the ceiling fan! All the dishes in the kitchen had smears and smudges of grime, and a few had been broken. The mirrors and windows had greasy, muddy fingerprints, and a few looked like they might have been licked! The kitchen had been dotted in splotches of goo and the stairs had trails of slime. Even the air looked dirty and smelled like unwashed monsters. When the parents arrived home from work, they finally agreed only monsters could have made such a mess, and it was impossible to blame the kids for this disaster.

The entire family pitched in to clean the house. After a few hours of cleaning and not looking like they made much progress at all, the family cleared a small area in the living room big enough for the family to sleep. The mother, the one who had left the basement window open for the tall, lumpy, purple monster to get in, had an idea. As the family settled down in their cleanish little patch of living room, she declared, "Family, we have done as good of a job as we possibly could."

The kids looked at the mess all around their cleanish, little circle.

"Are we going to move?" asked one of the kids.

"Nope," said their mother, "We tried. I don't think anyone could clean the house any better."

"I agree," the father said, catching on to his wife's idea, "If monsters can make this big of a mess, then only monsters can clean the house better." He added, "But, only if they take out the trash, too."

The kids did not know what their parents were up to. They fell asleep worrying they would have to live in a house that looked and smelled like a landfill.

The next morning, the family awoke and the house was still a tremendous mess. They left the mess behind and went to work and school. When they returned home at the end of the day, the house was spotless. Everything was where it should be. Beds were made. Clothes were washed, folded, and put neatly away. There were no stains anywhere, including the ones from before the monsters showed up. Windows and mirrors sparkled without a single streak or smudge. Dishes were washed and put away. Even the broken dishes were neatly glued together and sparkled like new. The house smelled lemony fresh. Outside, the lawn was mowed and the hedges were neatly trimmed. The trash and recyclables had been sorted and taken out to the proper bins. The family smiled and sighed with relief.

Afraid to make another mess before it could prove how clean the house could be, the tall, lumpy, purple monster and all its friends wandered away. The monster hoped it could find another nice family who might invite it in to stay. As proud as the monster was of cleaning the house so thoroughly, he hoped the new family would give it permission to make more messes.

Dad finished the story as he helped the kids put away their toys. He told them to brush their teeth and get ready for bed. After dressing in their pajamas and brushing their teeth, they returned to Dad to say goodnight.

"Are you going to watch TV?" Danny asked.

"No."

"Are you going to work some more?" Liz asked.

"Kind of. I have a couple more chores I would like to finish before Mom gets home. I want to start a load of dishes and clean up around the dinner table."

"Can we help?" Danny asked. "We want to help surprise Mom, too."

"And, we don't want any monsters getting ideas about making a mess," Liz added.

Dad agreed to let them help, even though it was a school night. Liz wiped down the dinner table and swept up the crumbs underneath the table, too. Danny helped put away the dishes. He helped fill the dishwasher again as Dad handed him rinsed off dishes.

Placing the last plate in the dishwasher, Mom walked through the door.

"Mommy's home!" Liz squealed.

"Hi kids! I'm so glad to be home! I missed you so much!"

Mom dropped her bags by the doorway, knelt down and embraced Liz and Danny in a big hug. She held onto them for a long time to make up for the days of missed hugs. Dad stood over them and smiled.

"Mommy, this weekend—," Liz started to say, before Dad interrupted her.

"Mommy just got home," Dad said to Liz. "We can tell her more about our week tomorrow."

Liz smiled and nodded. She and Danny gave Mom another

round of hugs.

When Ellie let go of the kids and stood up, Ben welcomed her home with a kiss. He said, "You're home early."

"I missed everyone so much, I caught an earlier flight," Ellie said. She looked at the time and asked, "Why are you kids still up? Shouldn't you be in bed?"

"We were helping Dad clean up," Liz said.

"Yeah, Dad made a monster-sized mess," Danny said, grinning.

"Don't believe him. I'm not that messy," Dad said.

"He made us stay up late cleaning, because he didn't want you to know how messy he is," Liz said, giggling.

"Don't believe her, either."

"Dad is really bad at lying, too," Liz said.

"The worst," Danny agreed.

"Don't believe them. The kids are full of stories," Dad said.

"Dad is full of stories, too," Liz said.

"Who knew?" Danny added.

"Now that is something I do believe," Mom said.

As happy as Danny and Liz felt with Mom home, hopefully they did not need to wait for Mom to leave town again to hear more of Dad's crazy stories.

ABOUT THE AUTHOR

Douglas Schwartz is a firehose of creativity. He juggles between developing websites, designing games, and writing ridiculous stories. Everything he creates is the real deal, and not created from AI. In fact, the only AI he believes in is Author Imagination, as it should be. He considers the struggle of figuring out how to craft his imagination into something real and sharable is a fantastic adventure.

Although this book is entirely fictional, both the short stories and the frame story, his wife and two kids (now adults) inspired this collection of *Dadtime Stories*.

For more of Douglas's shenanigans, please visit his website:

www.checkeredscissors.com

BEHIND THE DADTIME STORIES

Even though my kids are now adults, our time together while my wife was away on business trips or when she traveled with friends sparked the idea for this collection of unique tales.

I wanted to create original, modern tales based on lessons we tried to instill in our kids and concepts we struggled with as parents. Topics like encouraging the kids to try new foods, owning up to mistakes, or respecting other people's things and personal space. I made a list of such topics and then figured out stories to match. Some stories drastically changed from their original form.

Instead of providing only a collection of stories, I crafted the frame story around them. Danny and Liz are inspired by my kids, but completely fictional. I imagined how my kids might have reacted to these stories. Plus, I imagined what type of real-life scenarios might trigger such stories. The frame story is divided into four blocks of time, each occurring over four weekdays. These times are moments of the kids decompressing from returning home from school, eating dinner together as a family, followed by a bit of playtime before finally settling in for bedtime. My wife and I agreed to provide reliable structure when possible, which is why I crafted the story this way.

One of my greatest challenges for this book was how to format the stories surrounded by the frame story. I waffled all over the place, trying to make the collection look "right". Finally, I took inspiration from *I, Robot*, and how Asimov's frame story worked around each of the robot's tales.

The dad in the frame story contrasts with how I sometimes see other father figures. On TV, dads are typically oafish or strict. Some dads I have known were mostly hands-off. This book is for the other dads I know to be very much involved with their kids' lives. The dad in this collection is creative, silly, loving, calm, and understanding…the kinds of traits I express towards my own kids.

I hope you enjoyed reading this collection as much as I enjoyed crafting it.

Looking for more crazy Schwartz Stories?
Look no further!

Schwartz Stories for the little ones…

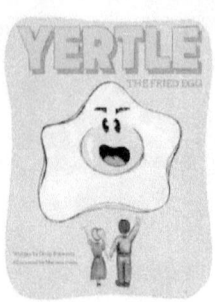

Schwartz Stories for everyone…

Find them at CheckeredScissors.com!

BLUEBERRY COOKIE-PIES

Did you read *The Shelf Life of Berries*?

Would you like to know how to bake your own Blueberry Cookie-Pies?

Follow this QR code to the recipe posted on my website!

If you try them, please let me know what you think.

Send me pictures of your take on this tasty treat!

Enjoy!

www.ingramcontent.com/pod-product-compliance
Lightning Source LLC
Chambersburg PA
CBHW021153130626
46554CB00005B/1797